Katie, Will
and the
Global Detectives

ROBERT P. RABBIT
BOOK ONE

Katie, Will and the Global Detectives

by GrandDad

Illustrated by
C. L. Hildebrandt

Published in the United States by the Larry Burkett Cancer
Research Foundation.

ISBN: 978-0-578-15499-2

This book is dedicated to the brave children who daily fight their battles against serious illness and injury.

PREFACE

We hope you enjoy the stories in this book, the first in the series of Robert P. Rabbit books, where you will meet some very interesting characters. The heroine of all the books is Katie, age ten, who has a sidekick, her brother Will, who is nine. Of course, the hero is the amazing rabbit named Robert P. Rabbit.

Join them in a series of short stories which take place the first year in which Robert P. Rabbit meets and gets to know his new friends as they share one exciting experience after another!

Katie has cancer, for which she is receiving treatments and which cause her to be dizzy and tired from time to time. She sometimes has to be in a wheelchair. But her illness does not deter her at all. She continues to have adventure after adventure, solving all sorts of mysteries with the help of Will and Robert P. Rabbit. She refuses to let her physical problems keep her from helping other people.

The books are written by Katies's GrandDad (See Author's Note in the back), and are owned, and distributed by The Larry Burkett Cancer Research Foundation.

INTRODUCTION

Robert P. Rabbit is the name of an amazing rabbit of very high character and intelligence who became a good friend to me and to my grandchildren.

But before I begin to tell you of our adventures, I should introduce myself. I live in a two-story house with my wife, who is called Polly by our nine grandchildren and therefore by the rest of us. I am GrandDad to everyone in my family, and I think all of them over ten years old think maybe I live a little "up in the clouds." That is because I spend a great deal of time talking to a furry white rabbit named Robert P. Rabbit, something none of the adults around me seem to be able to do. But it's not really my fault. He speaks to me, so it would be awfully rude of me not to speak to him, don't you think?

Anyway, after Robert P. Rabbit came into our lives, things just never were the same again for me or for my grandchildren, especially my granddaughter Katie. You see, Katie was my first grandchild to meet Robert P. Rabbit, and they became almost inseparable from their first day together. They just kept having adventure after adventure, and they always seemed to be just one step ahead of me.

Katie is ten years old and is a very wise, considerate, and loving child who is always thinking of others before she thinks of herself. She is sick a lot of the time, and sometimes sits in a wheelchair, but that never seems to slow the two of them down in the least.

But I think I am getting ahead of myself. I guess I should start at the beginning and let you see for yourself. Katie says it is always a good thing to start at the beginning, and I think she is right, so here goes!

CHAPTER ONE

WE MEET

We started the cool January day as we did most mornings, with a stroll around the public golf course in Chastain Park. Polly and I were dressed in light workout clothes, and we intended to make the three and a half mile loop in just under an hour. Because the path was somewhat steep in places, we set off from the parking lot at a very brisk pace and were soon well into the woods and away from the view of the road.

"How does your sore leg feel this morning, GrandDad?" Polly said. Since we have nine grandchildren who call me "GrandDad," she calls me that too, to avoid confusion when they are around. They call her Polly.

"I feel like this will be a good day," I said. Little did I know it would also be the day I would meet a friend who would bring unexpected adventures into our lives.

Only a few minutes into our walk, I spied something odd. "Hey, Polly," I said, "look at that ball of white fur over there." I pointed to what looked like a big ball of white cotton under a bush next to the trail.

"Looks dirty to me," said Polly. "Don't pick it up, you might catch something."

"What on earth could I catch from a ball of white cotton?" I said.

"Well, it might have germs on it," Polly said.

"Go ahead and pick it up," a voice said. I stopped and looked around to see who had spoken, but we were all alone on the trail. "What's the matter, you afraid of a ball of cotton?" the voice said.

"Did you hear that?" I asked Polly.

"Hear what?"

"The voice that told me to pick up the ball of cotton."

"You're hearing things. Now come on, let's get to walking before the morning crowds arrive," said Polly impatiently.

"No, I really did hear someone tell me to pick up that ball of cotton," I said.

"Well, okay," said Polly, "I'm going on ahead. You'll just have to catch up with me."

I moved closer to the bush and the ball of cotton. The voice spoke again. "Be careful how you handle me; I have a hurt leg." Surely someone was playing a joke on me. White balls of cotton just don't usually say things. There must be a hidden speaker somewhere in the bush. Then, as I leaned down to pick up the ball of cotton, I saw that it wasn't a ball of cotton at all. It was a rabbit. And not a stuffed rabbit, but a live one looking up at me with one blue eye and one pink eye that each glowed in the morning sun.

"Well, are you going to stand there like a knot on a log, or are you going to help?" said the rabbit, or whoever was speaking for the rabbit.

"Why sure," I said, as I could see that he had a hurt leg, bent out of shape and spotted with blood.

"Be careful," he said, "I told you I had a hurt leg." Now I knew something really weird was going on. He seemed to be talking, but he wasn't moving his lips, only twitching that little rabbit nose of his.

"Robert P. Rabbit," he said.

"What does that mean?" I said.

"What's the matter with you?" he said. "Didn't your mother teach you any manners? I'm introducing myself to you—I'm Robert P. Rabbit, and I would expect you to have the courtesy to tell me your name."

"GrandDad," I said, rather embarrassed that I was talking to a rabbit who was giving me a lesson in politeness. I don't know why I said "GrandDad." He was so small and helpless, and he reminded me of some of my grandchildren. So I guess "GrandDad" just naturally came out.

"You seem to be talking to me," I said, "but I don't see your lips moving." I still thought maybe someone was playing a giant trick on me.

"That's because I am speaking to you with my mind. We rabbits don't make a racket with our voices—it's such a waste of energy."

"Can you read my mind?" I said.

"Of course not," said the rabbit. "I can't unless you throw your thoughts from your mind to mine, but you obviously are not smart enough to do that, so you will just have to keep using your voice until you figure it all out."

I could tell that this Robert P. Rabbit was getting the best of me, so I decided it was best to play along. "What happened to you?" I asked.

"I was riding in the back of a turnip truck," he said. "When I got to Atlanta, I jumped out as the truck slowed down, and I hurt my leg when I hit the pavement. I don't believe anything is ever an accident, so I think maybe this was supposed to happen so you could find me."

"Hmmm. That's very interesting, but I've got to keep walking," I said. "My wife has gone on ahead, so I need to catch up with her."

"Sounds good to me," he said. "Just so you fix up my leg."

"Oh I can't do that," I said, "but I'll take you to a veterinarian and he can help you."

"No you won't, big boy," said the rabbit emphatically. "I know about veterinarians. They put rabbits in cages and no thank you. I don't want to be in a cage. You can just take me to your house—you do live in a house, don't you?"

"Of course I live in a house, but I'll have to ask my wife first."

"Are you the man of the house, or is she in charge?"

I wasn't sure I liked where this conversation was going, so I changed the subject. "When we catch up, you can just tell her yourself that you want to come home with us."

"Sorry again, big boy, but she won't hear me. She doesn't have THE MARK," he said.

"What do you mean she doesn't have 'THE MARK'?"

"Well for some reason only a handful of you humans can hear us special rabbits speak, and there are only a handful of us special rabbits. We can tell which humans can hear us by THE MARK on the side of their head just in front of their right ear. It glows, but you humans can't see it, so you don't even know who you are. I saw THE MARK when you stopped on the trail. That's why I spoke to you."

"Well, Robert," I said, "I…"

"The name is Robert P. Rabbit, if you please."

"That's what I said, Robert."

"No, it's not. When addressing me you shall always use my full name—Robert P. Rabbit—if you please."

"Why?" I said.

"That's another story for another time," he said. "Now pick me up and let's get going before I get taken by a fox, or something worse, like a ten year-old-boy."

So I picked him up, and off we went to catch up with Polly.

CHAPTER TWO

HOME IS WHERE THE HEART IS

Well, I caught up with Polly on the trail fairly easily. I think she had stopped up ahead to watch me and didn't start off again until she saw me pick up Robert P. Rabbit and come after her at a fairly high speed.

"Slow down, big boy," Robert P. Rabbit said. "It hurts my leg when you bounce"

"Okay," I said. "We've almost caught up to Polly anyway."

As we approached Polly, she said, "Oh GrandDad, what are you doing picking up that dirty ball of cotton?"

"I wish she would stop calling me a dirty ball of cotton," said Robert P. Rabbit testily.

"Well she hasn't had a good look at you yet," I said. "It isn't a dirty piece of cotton, Polly; it's a rabbit with a hurt leg."

"A rabbit!" she squealed. "That's even worse than a dirty piece of cotton. Put it down before you get rabies."

"I'm not going to take many more of these insults," said Robert P. Rabbit.

"She doesn't mean any harm," I said.

"Who doesn't mean any harm?" said Polly.

"Sorry," I said, "I wasn't talking to you."

"Then who on earth were you talking to?"

"Oh, I was just talking to myself," I lied.

"Not a good start, big boy," said Robert P. Rabbit. "I can't wait to see how you get out of this one."

"We really need to help this poor rabbit, Polly," I said. "If we leave him here, some big animal will probably eat him."

"How do you know it's a he?" said Polly. "And what in the world do you know about fixing rabbits?"

"I'll just go online and look up fixing hurt rabbits. I'll find something," I said.

We argued and talked and argued some more all around the path and back to our car, and all the time Robert P. Rabbit kept interrupting me and making Polly believe I was crazy. But Polly saw that I had made up my mind to help this rabbit. As we got into the car, I wrapped Robert P. Rabbit carefully in my jacket and laid him on the backseat.

"What if he jumps up to the front seat, GrandDad? We'll have a wreck."

"He can't do that, remember? He has a hurt leg."

At home, Polly said I should wash him off with a hose in the backyard, but I wanted to use our bathtub. We settled on the deep sink in the laundry room. As I examined his leg, I could tell it was just a sprain, since it only hurt him when he tried to hop on it or when I moved it from side to side.

"Be careful, big boy," he said. "I'm not a fish. We rabbits are not fond of water."

"You're kidding," I said. "I didn't know that."

"Have you ever seen a rabbit swimming in the river or wading in the pond or dancing in the rain? Have you ever even seen a rabbit with an umbrella? Of course not. We don't have umbrellas because unlike you humans, we have the good sense not to go out in the rain in the first place. So watch yourself with the water, big boy," he said.

By the time he had finished with his tirade about the water, I had finished washing him and had taken a good look at his leg. "I think you have a sprain," I said, "so I'm going to wrap your leg in an Ace bandage."

"This is getting pretty bad, GrandDad," said Polly, walking into the room just then. "Talking to the rabbit like it was a person. I've been listening to you and you seem a little ridiculous."

"Well I've certainly heard you talk to Pepper plenty of times," I said. Pepper is Polly's cat. I was proud of myself for coming up with such a quick response.

"That's different. Pepper is a pet—part of the family."

"Well you go ahead and keep talking to Pepper, and I'll talk to this rabbit," I said.

"Pretty good, big boy," said Robert P. Rabbit.

"Thanks," I said.

"Thanks for what?" said Polly. "And how do you know that rabbit is a he," she said.

"Well he has a boy's name," I said, not quite catching myself in time. "Anyway," I quickly added, "I've given him a boy's name—so he is a boy for now."

"Oh no," she said, "now you've gone and named him. I see what's coming. You're going to want to keep him and where in the world will you put him and what will you feed him and what if he messes up the house and what if he has a disease and what if Pepper doesn't like him?" And Polly stormed out of the laundry room.

"Does she always talk that much?" said Robert P. Rabbit. "And how can she ask so many questions without waiting for any answers?"

"Well it's just her way of getting in all she wants to say so she can possibly leave me so confused I'll go along with whatever she decides," I said.

"Okay," said Robert P. Rabbit. "If she is going to object to my being in the house while my leg heals, this calls for some special strategy. You just do what I tell you to do, and she'll be all right. Trust me."

For the next few minutes I could tell that Robert P. Rabbit was deep in thought and that I shouldn't do anything to interrupt him. Then all of a sudden he looked up at me and said, "We'll go with plan C."

"What's Plan C?" I said.

"Well, I usually have several plans for any situation," said Robert P. Rabbit, "and after giving them all a great deal of thought, and considering how everyone involved will react, and what the results of each plan will be, I select the one that will be best for everyone concerned. In this case, it's plan C," he said.

"What happened to Plan A and Plan B?" I said.

"They'll never do. Plan A is too risky and Plan B will make her mad, and we don't want that. So of course we go with plan C."

"Of course," I said, "I hadn't thought of it that way." So plan C it was, and what a good plan it turned out to be, if I do say so myself.

"Take me to the cat, big boy," he said.

"No, we better not do that. Once, when we brought another cat into the house, she went crazy, running around the room hissing and scratching and making everyone miserable."

"Just take me to Pepper," he said impatiently, paying no attention to the dangers I had just described.

So off we went from the laundry room to Pepper's favorite place, Polly's chair in the sunroom. Robert P. Rabbit said, "Put me down on the floor in front of the chair."

"I don't think that's a good idea," I said.

"Just do what I say, big boy," said Robert P. Rabbit.

So I put him down in front of Pepper's chair and stepped back, waiting for the fireworks to start and wondering if I would be able to fix the injuries Robert P. Rabbit would receive from Pepper. As I expected, as soon as she spotted the rabbit, Pepper stood up on all fours, arched her back, and struck the "Halloween cat" pose calculated to frighten even the bravest of potential enemies. But then an amazing thing happened. Robert P. Rabbit began to inch closer to the chair, twitching his nose and waving his ears. As he did so, Pepper began to relax and moved her head from side to side slowly, as if she were looking for someone to tell her what was happening.

She settled back down in her chair. Just then Robert P. Rabbit hopped up onto the chair using his one good leg and landed right beside Pepper. Miracle of miracles, Pepper snuggled up to Robert P. Rabbit and purred as she licked Robert P. Rabbit's hurt leg. I couldn't believe my eyes.

I had to find Polly and tell her the news. I found her in the laundry room.

"What did you do with that rabbit?" she asked. "I hope you took him out to the garage where he belongs."

"No," I said smugly. "I took him into the sunroom to meet Pepper."

"You did what?" she screamed. "Quick, we've got to save him. Pepper will tear him apart!" She rushed through the kitchen and into the sunroom.

What she saw stopped her right in her tracks. Pepper and Robert P. Rabbit were curled up together into one great big cat and white rabbit ball, sleeping. "Oh my goodness," she sighed. "Pepper must love him a lot. She would never curl up and sleep with anyone she didn't love." I took this to mean that Pepper only tolerated me but didn't love me, because Pepper would never sleep on my side of the bed. No matter, though, Polly could see that Pepper and Robert P. Rabbit were going to be fast friends.

"Well, I guess the rabbit can call this home for the time being since Pepper has accepted him," Polly said.

"Yes," I said, "it is easy to see that Pepper and Robert P. Rabbit are two pets who are not just side by side, but are heart to heart, and home is where the heart is."

When Polly turned around, Robert P. Rabbit looked at me and winked.

CHAPTER THREE

ROBERT P. RABBIT
MEETS KATIE

For the next several weeks, we all got to know each other better. Robert P. Rabbit even took over Polly's chair. Pepper now had to ask permission to join him on the chair. Still, it was plain to see that they had become fast friends, even playing games together like tag and leap frog, as Robert P. Rabbit's leg healed more each day.

Robert P. Rabbit was very curious about everything. "What is this?" he would say, pointing to an object, "and what is it for?"

"That is a telephone," I would reply. "We can use it to talk to each other when we are miles apart."

"You don't say," he would say. "And what is that?"

"That is a microwave oven. We use it to cook things quickly when we don't want to fire up the stove."

"You don't say. And what is that small square object?"

"That is an emergency signal machine. If Polly or I are home alone and we need help, all we have to do is touch that red button and help comes right away."

"You don't say," he would say each time, not really as a question, but more as if he were proud of me for knowing what things are, like maybe he knew all along but wanted to make sure I knew. This went on for hours and hours until I had described everything in the house. I got the feeling that he was testing me.

Of course, Polly thought I had lost my mind talking so much to a rabbit, but she did not bother me about it anymore, as she had many more important things to think about. Our granddaughter, Katie, was coming to stay with us. Robert P. Rabbit knew something was afoot, as Polly spent many hours fixing up our daughter's old bedroom with new wall hangings, new curtains, a new bedspread, and new books on the shelves. She kept the door closed so that neither Pepper nor Robert P. Rabbit could get into the room and perhaps mess something up. I could tell that this made Robert P. Rabbit very upset, as he was becoming the King of the Hill. The idea that someone more important than him was coming to live with us was more than he could stand.

I later found out that Robert P. Rabbit had a special power to do amazing things that were not possible for normal rabbits. Using this special talent when I wasn't looking, Robert P. Rabbit set out to make certain that Katie would know she was not welcome. He snuck into her room and set the alarm by her bed to go off at 2:00 a.m. He put glasses of water under the bed that he could pour into her bed at night to make us think that she had wet the bed. He put sand on the blades of the ceiling fan so that when she turned it on, sand would shoot all over her, the bed, and the room. He even hid bugs in cardboard boxes under her bed so he could put them into her clothes at night to scare her in the morning.

The day came when Katie arrived. We brought her into her new room. Robert P. Rabbit and Pepper were put into the laundry room to be out of the way, but after Katie was settled in her bed, I took Robert P. Rabbit to meet Katie. I put him down just inside the door so Katie could see him first.

Robert P. Rabbit was ready to spring up to her bed and give her a good scare. But just as he took one hop forward, he looked up at Katie and froze. With both front feet in the air and his ears flat down on his back, he just stood there and looked.

"What's the matter?" I said. He didn't answer, so I asked him again, "What's the matter?"

"She has THE MARK," he whispered to me.

"What?" I said.

"THE MARK—like you. I can talk to her, and any-one with THE MARK is supposed to be treated as a friend, a member of the family. You didn't tell me she had THE MARK," he said.

"You forgot, I can't see THE MARK," I said.

He didn't answer me. He just hopped slowly forward and said, "Hello, Katie. I'm Robert P. Rabbit."

"Hello, Robert P. Rabbit. I'm Katie. I'm so glad to meet you. Are you going to be my friend?" said Katie.

"I'd like to be your friend, if you'll let me," said Robert P. Rabbit. I had never heard him so humble. It was like he knew Katie was more special than anyone he had ever met.

"I have lots of things to tell you," said Katie, "and I think we will have lots of fun together right after I take my nap. Come get in bed with me and we can keep each other warm," said Katie. So Robert P. Rabbit jumped up in the bed with Katie and stayed right next to her until she was fast asleep.

"What do you think of Katie?" I asked him after Katie was asleep.

"She's sick, isn't she?" he asked.

"Yes. She has cancer."

"What's that?"

"It's a disease that eats you up from the inside, but we are going to try to stop it. There are no hospitals where she lives in Tallulah Falls, so we brought her here so she could be close to Children's Hospital, which is only a mile and a half away."

I had never seen Robert P. Rabbit so quiet. He fixed all the bad things he had planned to do. He told me about them and asked forgiveness, and I told him I certainly would forgive him, but Katie was the one he needed to tell. When Katie woke up they had a long, long talk, ending with Katie giving him a big hug, showing that she forgave him. I knew she would. Katie was like that.

Before bedtime that night, I heard Robert P. Rabbit tell her that he would be her best friend.

"No," she said. "My cousin, Emily, is my best friend. I have brothers and a sister and another cousin, Mary Brooks, who are friends too, but they are family, so I don't make them get into the friend line. But Emily is both, a part of my family, and my best friend," she said.

"Well, I'll be your second best friend, or even your third best friend if you want," he said. "A real friend doesn't care if he is first, second, third, or fifteenth best friend. He is just glad to be one of your friends. That's the way I want to be, Katie, anywhere in the line," said Robert P. Rabbit.

Katie hugged him and said, "You can be my second best friend, Robert P. Rabbit." And that is how Robert P. Rabbit met our dear, sweet Katie.

CHAPTER FOUR

KATIE'S FIRST VISIT TO CHILDREN'S HOSPITAL

It was late winter when we first took Katie to the hospital for some tests and treatments. We were all very worried, but Katie was her usual cheerful self and didn't seem to be worried at all. Her mom (our daughter Wendy), her dad Carl, her brothers Will and Parker, and her sister Arielle, came to live with us too, although Arielle had to go back with her dad to Tallulah Falls for school during the week. They made quite a group in the house, and they were all curious about Robert P. Rabbit. Although Will and Parker both had THE MARK, Robert P. Rabbit thought it best not to communicate with them just yet, and Katie and I honored that decision.

After arriving at her room at the Children's Hospital, Katie immediately began asking for Robert P. Rabbit. Because there was so much to do to check Katie into the hospital, we had left him at home.

"But GrandDad," she said, "Robert P. Rabbit can go in-animate whenever he wants to."

I didn't even know Katie knew such a big word, much less what it means.

Seeing the quizzical look on my face, Katie said, "What I mean, GrandDad, is that he can look to everyone like he is a stuffed rabbit, and not a real rabbit at all. Oh please, can you bring him here?"

"We'll see, honey," I said doubtfully. Of course that wasn't good enough for Katie. She made me promise I would ask him about what he could do.

So when I got home, I asked Robert P. Rabbit just exact-ly what Katie was talking about, and Robert P. Rabbit ex-plained it to me.

"You see, big boy, I have more tricks up my furry lit-tle paw than Bayer has aspirin. With just a flop of our ears, we rabbits who have the gift can appear as if we are simply stuffed toy animals. We are just like the toys in the *Toy Story* movies. When people come around, all of the *Toy Story* char-acters immediately become inanimate, appearing to be just manufactured toys. And they stay that way until the people leave. But we gifted rabbits can do one better. We can be in-animate and appear to be a stuffed rabbit, or we can come fully to life, whichever we want to do—whether people are present or not. We can do it any time we like. See?"

Robert P. Rabbit wiggled his ears in a funny motion on his head and flopped down on the ground. I couldn't believe my eyes. He looked just like a fluffy white toy rabbit. But then he blinked at me and grinned. "So what do you think of that, big boy?" he said.

"Great!" I said. Now I could take him to the hospital to see Katie. However, before I did so, I decided I had better come clean with Polly. Even though she hadn't asked me many questions, I knew by the way she looked at me that she thought I was going crazy. So I sat her down and explained everything that had been happening over the past few weeks. I told her about THE MARK and about how Katie and I could communicate with Robert P. Rabbit; I told her how Robert P. Rabbit could make Pepper into a calm and docile cat; and I told her how Robert P. Rabbit could become like a stuffed rabbit whenever he wanted to. "I'm sure he will have even more surprises in store for us in the future," I finished.

Polly just looked at me doubtfully until she saw Robert P. Rabbit become exactly like a soft, cuddly stuffed rabbit, right before her eyes. After that she never questioned me again, and she even grew to appreciate all the wonderful things Robert P. Rabbit brought into Katie's life.

I had no trouble at all carrying Robert P. Rabbit under my arm right past the receptionist on the first floor, past the nurse's station on Katie's floor, and on into her room. She squealed with delight when she saw him and began to tell him all about her tests and treatments. Robert P. Rabbit seemed to know all about what she was going through—like maybe he had known other children with cancer. I made it a point to ask him about it later.

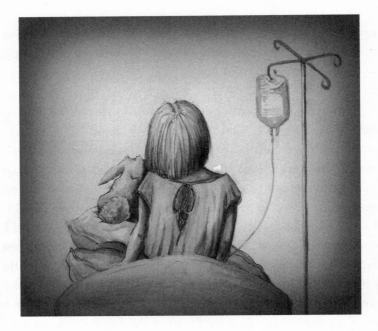

Katie took Robert P. Rabbit all around her floor and introduced him to all the nurses and to all of the other children. Katie's giving and loving nature made her an instant friend to everyone she met. She always thought of others first before she thought of herself. In fact, within a day or two of arriving at the hospital, Katie had received a dozen or more stuffed animals from many of her friends.

"GrandDad," she said to me, "I have so many wonderful animals, and many of the children on my floor don't have any animals at all. Can I give my animals away?"

"Certainly," I said, "but make sure it is okay with the nurses and the parents of the children first." In three days, Katie had given away thirteen stuffed animals. She was soon asking everyone who visited her if they had any extras so she could give them away, too. By the end of her first stay in the hospital, every child on her floor had six or seven stuffed animals, with more on the counter of the nurse's station.

That is, all except one little boy named Eddie.

"GrandDad," she said, "Eddie didn't want any of the animals. He said all he wants is a black bear cub, and no one has given me a black bear cub."

What a strange request, I thought. There were giraffes, elephants, monkeys, and even a raccoon, but he didn't want any of them. So I brought it up to Robert P. Rabbit, who had visited Eddie with Katie on several occasions.

"You have to understand," said Robert P. Rabbit, who always seemed to know just what was going on all around him, "Eddie's mom has four young children at home to take care of, and his dad is a farmer who is in the middle of planting season. They live in Hiawassee, Georgia, a long ways away. They can't stay very long when they come, so Eddie is all alone a lot of the time.

"At home, just before Eddie came to the hospital for treatment," said Robert P. Rabbit, "a mother black bear and her cub came down from the mountains to their farm to look for food, and Eddie put out blueberries that his mom had gotten from their bushes. Every day, one of the cubs came right up to Eddie's bedroom window to eat the blueberries off the windowsill while Eddie talked to him. Now he misses the cub."

So Robert P. Rabbit and Katie came up with an idea. Katie's brother Will had a stuffed black bear cub, but they knew that Will would not want to part with it. So the next day, when Will came to the hospital to visit Katie, she told him she wanted to see Blackie, Will's black bear cub.

When Will came with the bear cub, she took Will all over the floor to meet all the other children. Finally she took him to Eddie's room. Eddie lit up and smiled when he saw Blackie. "Can I hold him?" he asked. Will let him hold Blackie for a while. Eddie looked very sad when Will took Blackie back and they left the room.

When they got back to Katie's room, she told Will about Eddie's real bear cub back home. "Anyone can give castoff toys to another child," Katie said, "but the best gift of all is to give someone a toy you really love yourself."

Will thought for a minute. "Do you think I should give Blackie to Eddie?"

"Well," said Katie, "if you did that, I would think you were the most generous and giving brother in the whole wide world, and you would forever be one of my heroes."

Will left the room without another word. After a while he came back, and there were tears in his eyes.

"Why are you crying?" Katie asked.

"I am so happy to see how much Blackie means to Eddie," Will said. "Eddie smiled from ear to ear, and he wouldn't stop telling Blackie all about the hospital, the nurses, the doctors, and even you, Katie." Will added, "Katie, I have never felt so good in all my life." Robert P. Rabbit winked his pink eye at Katie, and Katie winked back.

CHAPTER FIVE

ROBERT P. RABBIT SAVES THE FAMILY

From the time Katie first arrived at our house, she and Robert P. Rabbit were nearly inseparable. Polly even let him sleep in Katie's bed. But he didn't stay there all night. For some reason, Robert P. Rabbit wanted to be sure we were all safe at night. He began to get up every night around two or three o'clock in the morning and hop all around the house. How he woke himself up to do this I'll never know, but he did.

"What are you doing this for?" I asked him one day.

"Well there is no way that lazy cat Pepper is going to check things out during the middle of the night, and you are usually snoring like a buzz saw, so it is obviously up to me to see that everything is okay in the house. I check to be sure you locked all the doors, turned off all the lights, and didn't leave any windows open."

"You're wasting your time," I said.

"We'll see," he said.

One warm night during dinner, we opened the door to the sunroom for the pleasant night air. After dinner, we forgot that it was open, and after a stirring game of Dominos, we all went upstairs to bed.

Late that night while Robert P. Rabbit was making his rounds downstairs, he knew something was wrong. The sunroom door was open much wider than we had left it earlier in the evening. Peering around the corner from the living room, he saw a large man dressed in black with a ski mask on his face. He had a big bag into which he was putting the silverware from the kitchen cabinet. He had already put the TV by the door.

Robert P. Rabbit had to think quickly and move fast. First he pushed the panic button on the emergency alert device that I had shown him. Then, as the burglar moved to the dining room to get the silver tea and coffee pots from the table, Robert P. Rabbit quietly closed the sunroom door and pushed a big chair in front it. Taking some clothesline from the laundry room, he tied it back and forth between the legs of some of the barstool chairs in the kitchen and across the room to the legs of the chair in front of Polly's desk. He then put some glass vases on the chairs.

Robert P. Rabbit watched as the burglar began to walk upstairs. As soon as he was at the top of the stairs, Robert P. Rabbit opened the front door very quietly. The burglar was so intent on figuring out which room was which that he didn't notice what Robert P. Rabbit was doing. At that moment, Robert P. Rabbit turned on the radio in the den as loud as it would go. It was tuned to a newscast station, so there was a lot of talking. Hearing the voices, the burglar came flying down the stairs to run away.

He ran through the dining room and into the kitchen, trying to make it to the door in the sunroom. He tripped over the ropes Robert P. Rabbit had put out. The glass vases came crashing to the floor, shattering into a million pieces and making quite a racket. Seeing the sunroom door was closed and blocked by a chair, the burglar ran toward the front of the house. He noticed that the front door was open (as Robert P. Rabbit had left it that way), so, without thinking, he lunged through the door to make his escape to the front yard.

Unfortunately for him, he landed right into the arms of Sandy Springs' finest fireman, who had responded to the emergency call put in by Robert P. Rabbit. The fireman wrestled him to the ground and tied him up.

All the commotion woke us up, and I darted downstairs to see what was happening. The fireman had called the police, and they quickly came and put the burglar securely in custody. "Do you always set that kind of a rope trap for burglars in your kitchen?" they asked. Polly said she didn't remember any ropes being tied to the chair legs, and she certainly didn't remember putting any vases onto the chairs, but she was not in a mood to question why it was done, because the results were so good.

Of course, the first thing we did was check on Katie since her mother and brothers had gone back to Tallulah Falls, and she was fast asleep with Robert P. Rabbit curled up by her side. I pretended like I didn't know what he had done, but I couldn't stop myself from saying, "Thanks, Robert P. Rabbit," the next day when I saw him. He didn't say anything right away, but twitched his nose like he does sometimes when he is especially pleased with himself.

That night, right after reading a story to Katie and saying her prayers with her, I said, "Goodnight, Katie. I love you," and, "Goodnight, Robert P. Rabbit."

Katie said, "Goodnight GrandDad. I love you, too." All Robert P. Rabbit said was, "You're welcome."

CHAPTER SIX

A TRIP TO THE SNOW

For spring break that year, we decided to take Katie to Colorado to snow ski. Of course, to get there we had to fly, which was going to be quite an experience for Robert P. Rabbit. This being the first time Robert P. Rabbit ever flew, he had a lot of questions.

"Do we get wings all of a sudden to help us fly?" he asked.

"No," said Katie. "We will get into an airplane, and it will do the flying for us."

"The little metal things I see in the sky all the time? How can we all get into one of those when they look so small?"

"Yes, those are airplanes. They are a lot bigger when you see them on the ground than when you see them so far away in the air. So don't worry; we will all fit in the plane."

"OK," he said, "assuming we can all get into the thing, what makes it go up into the air? Does it flap its wings like a bird?"

"GrandDad, I think you need to answer that one," said Katie.

Well, it had been a long time since I had to answer that question, so I needed a little time to think it through. It is kind of amazing that something as big as an airplane can fly through the air with what seems like very little effort, especially after 200 or so people get inside of it and all of their luggage is also put inside. It is really nothing short of a miracle, but I knew I couldn't just say that to Robert P. Rabbit; he would never accept that as the only explanation. So I did my best to remember back to my high school physics course and to what I first learned about the science of air pressure, and I blurted out my simplest answer. "Air pressure keeps the plane up," I said.

"That doesn't make much sense," said Robert P. Rabbit. "What do you mean by air pressure, and where does it come from, and who is in charge of air pressure, and what happens if you run out of air pressure?" he added.

I could see that this was going to be a little more difficult than I first imagined, so I continued.

"You see, the air that is all around us exerts pressure on everything it touches. So long as we are fairly stable and not moving too fast, the air pressure all around us is uniform, and doesn't affect our position relative to the ground. In addition, even if we are going at a fairly high rate of speed, if the air moves around us on all sides evenly, we will still not be affected. A car moving very fast down the highway does not rise off the ground because of the uniform movement of the air all around it. But an airplane is made differently. It has two very long wings on each side that are shaped so that when the airplane moves very fast, instead of the air going all around the wings evenly, the air has to go over the top of the wings, and not so much under the wings. This makes the air pressure under the wings much greater than the air pressure on top of the wings, and the air under the wings then pushes the wings up, and as the wings go up, it carries the entire plane with it, and it flies."

By the time I finished explaining, Robert P. Rabbit wasn't interested the least in physics. I sighed with relief to get to an easier question.

"When we are up that high, will we be able to see people and animals on the ground? Will I be able to wave at my friends on the ground? Will they be able to see me?" he asked.

"No," I said, "you will be so high up the things on the ground will be too small. You won't be able to tell what is a person, what is an animal, and what is a tree."

"Phooey," he said. "None of my friends have ever been up in an airplane, and if I can't see them and they can't see me, they will never believe I have flown."

"That's OK, Robert P. Rabbit," said Katie. "I'll tell them, and they will believe me."

With that we began to prepare for the trip. We had lots of packing to do, and Katie had to decide what she was going to take and what she would leave behind, which always seems to be a big dilemma for girls. For us boys it's easy. Some blue jeans, some shirts—whichever are currently clean—a sweater or two, underwear, gloves, and a jacket. How easy is that? But for girls it is a much different affair. What color will look good with my new coat? What will the other girls in Colorado be wearing? Which sweater looks good with which pants? Do I wear the same thing at least twice, or do I need a different outfit for each day? And on and on until they finally decide that they just don't have anything to wear, and they must go shopping right away before all the new clothes in the department stores are gone.

"GrandDad, how cold will it be?" asked Katie.

"I don't know for certain, but the Weather App tells me it will be pretty cold," I said.

"Wow GrandDad. We are going to need warm clothes, and gloves or mittens, and ear muffs, and I'm going to need to find a coat for Robert P. Rabbit!" she shouted.

"You had better talk to him about that," I said.

Off she went to find a coat for Robert P. Rabbit. I could tell from the look on his little bunny face that a coat was the last thing he wanted for this trip. So instead of going with her, he headed for his favorite chair to take his afternoon nap. We all knew that when he is taking one of his famous afternoon naps, he is not to be disturbed for anything unless the house is on fire, the roof has fallen in, or there is something that Katie needs right away.

In the meantime, Katie had gone into the upstairs dress-up closet and was busy looking for a warm coat for Robert P. Rabbit. Most everything she found was much too big for him. So she thought and thought, and finally a light bulb went off in her head. She knew just where to look. She ran to the playroom, to a box that contained her doll clothes. She was sure that one of her dolls must have a warm coat that would be just the right size for Robert P. Rabbit. She found three that were definite possibilities. One was a wonderful red sweater that seemed just his size. She could roll up the sleeves, and that would leave plenty of room for his paws to walk.

The second one was a bright pink jacket made of polyester that looked like fur. It zipped up the front, which might be a problem, but she wasn't too worried; she knew he wouldn't choose this one anyway. The third one was the one she liked most. It was dark brown, and it wasn't really even a doll's coat, but something else all together. So she put all three into a small box, with the red one on top, the bright pink one next, and the dark brown one on the bottom, and off she went to find Robert P. Rabbit.

By then he was almost finished with his nap, but she had to wake him, so she poked him in his furry little tummy and said in a very loud voice, "Wake up, wake up, wake up!" which he could not help but do after so loud a greeting, and with such a sudden poke in his tummy.

"What's going on?" he said. "Is the house on fire?"

"No, silly," said Katie. "GrandDad says it is going to be

really cold in Colorado when we go skiing, and we are going to have to dress warmly with coats and gloves and hats and scarves and such, and I'm worried about you, so I've found something for you to wear to keep you warm."

"Calm down, Katie," he said. "Don't you know that my warm fur is all I need to keep me warm even in the coldest weather? In fact, where I grew up in the mountains of North Georgia we had snow every year, and my brothers and sister and I loved to play in it all day long. We never got cold, and the hawks and bobcats and pumas could hardly see us as our fur is the same color as the snow. So Katie, I don't think I will need any coats or sweaters or mittens. I'll be OK as I am."

Katie didn't listen. She had made up her mind that Robert P. Rabbit was going to have a coat, and that was that. So she came up to his chair with the box and set it down in front of him.

"Here's a beautiful red sweater that should fit you perfectly. It belongs to my doll, Roberta, so that should please you since her name is so close to your name," Katie said.

Robert P. Rabbit could see he was going to have to humor Katie and pretend for now he would agree to wear something, but he certainly wasn't going to wear a coat that was made for a girl doll. He said, "Katie, red just doesn't go with the color of my fur. If I wore that, I would be red and white and look like a Christmas candy cane. Don't you have something else?"

"Well," said Katie, "I do have this wonderful bright pink jacket. It is made of polyester, so it looks just like fur, and it is just the right size."

"Oh dear," thought Robert P. Rabbit, "this one is worse than the first one. Things seem to be going down hill." So he said, "Katie, if I wore that, people would laugh at me. They would call me names, like Pretty Boy, or Girly Rabbit, or Pretty Pink Baby, or something even worse. I can't wear that."

"OK," said Katie, "I do have one more, but I'm not sure

you'll wear it. Remember Uncle Eric and Aunt Callie have a dog named Bridger that I really love? Well, they gave me a stuffed dog that looks just like Bridger, and it has a dark brown cover up that is just your size. But I'm not sure you want to wear a jacket that looks like something Bridger would wear, since you're not a dog."

To wear something that a dog Katie really loved might wear would please him to no end, so he said, "OK, if that's all you have, I guess I'll wear this one—but only if it is really cold."

Of course that is what Katie had planned all along. Now they could get on with the rest of the planning for the trip.

The two of them spent many hours talking and packing, and talking and repacking. Katie was only allowed one small roller board suitcase, so she had to be very selective about what she could fit into it. It had a picture on the side of her favorite princess, the fiery Rapunzel from the movie *Tangled*, so she didn't mind that it was a little small.

"Should I take my white jacket or my pink one?" she seemed to ask of no one. "Should I take my blue scarf or my pink one? Should I take my red gloves or my pink ones? Should I take my black socks or my pink ones?" This went on for hours, and it never mattered which one Robert P. Rabbit suggested she take, because the pink always won out. Robert P. Rabbit told her that if she really didn't want his opinion, she shouldn't even bother to ask, but that didn't seem to faze Katie. She kept asking the same question and kept coming to the same conclusion: pink. When I passed her room and made the comment, "Katie, that sure is a lot of pink you are packing," she responded very quickly, "GrandDad, there can NEVER be too much pink," with special emphasis on the word NEVER.

For Robert P. Rabbit, Katie was allowed to take a special little backpack that not only would have his new Bridger coat in it, but also would have space enough for him to settle into it, while at the same time allowing him to look out over everything around him to be sure things were going as they should. On the airplane, when others might be looking, he would make himself inanimate, and it would not look strange at all, since many ten-year-old girls bring their favorite stuffed animal on the plane with them. After meeting Robert P. Rabbit, I always wondered if the other stuffed animals I saw on planes were as amazing as he was, but he assured me that none of them could possibly be as amazing, so I could stop wondering.

Before we could consider ourselves ready for the trip, Katie made sure we had carrots for Robert P. Rabbit, so he would have something special to eat if he got hungry. Finally the morning came to head to the airport for the noon flight to Denver, Colorado. As we were loading the car Katie asked, "Aren't you bringing my wheelchair?"

"No," I said "The airline will have one for you as soon as we arrive at the airport, and they will push you all the way to the plane. Someone else will meet us at the plane when we land and push you all the way to the rental car bus. Then we've rented a wheelchair in Denver, which we will keep until we fly home."

"Why do you still need a wheelchair?" asked Robert P. Rabbit. "You seem well enough to me not to need one, and you don't always use one at home."

"It's because the cancer is in my head, and even though the radiation has made me better, I still get dizzy sometimes, and they don't want me to fall when that happens. At home I know where to hold on to things, but when I'm out, I can't always be sure there is something I can grab if I need it, so it is safer for me to be in the wheelchair. Besides, I get very tired if I have to stay walking for very long."

"Also," she added, "how many other people get to ride almost everywhere they go and get so much special treatment when they get there? There are special places for me at church, at the movies, at restaurants, and they even have special ramps at corners where I can get from the sidewalk into the road with no trouble at all." Katie was very proud that she was treated so special, and she continued to tell Robert P. Rabbit all of the benefits of being in a wheelchair.

At the airport we parked and joined Wendy and Will, who were going with us. When we arrived at the gate where the plane was, we were just in time to hear them announce that those needing special assistance could board the plane right away.

"See," said Katie to Robert P. Rabbit, "I told you they would treat me special. We are the first ones on the plane."

"No, we're not," said Robert P. Rabbit. "The pilots and the flight attendants got on before we did. I'm sure they are more important to the other people on the plane than we are."

"I guess you're right," she said. "There is always someone more important than we are, so we shouldn't think too much of ourselves. Then we won't be disappointed."

"That's good thinking," he said.

All this time, Will was staring at Robert P. Rabbit with his mouth open. "What's going on?" he asked. He had just figured out he could hear everything Robert P. Rabbit was saying. He wanted to know everything. Was Katie really talking to the rabbit, and was the rabbit really talking to her? Did he really hear what he thought he heard? So while they waited for the other passengers to board the plane, Katie told Will all about Robert P. Rabbit and the amazing things that had happened since he had come to live with her. Will had many questions he wanted to ask, but for now he was just excited that he was going to be able to talk to a rabbit. It was like living in a Disney movie.

We all settled into our seats, and almost before we were out of sight of the Atlanta skyline, Katie, Robert P. Rabbit, and Will were fast asleep. Before we got to Denver, I knew I would wake them up so they could look out the window and see parts of the United States they had never seen before. But for now things were quiet, and I needed some rest myself.

CHAPTER SEVEN

THE ROCKY MOUNTAINS AND SNOW

Katie and Will sat with their faces plastered up against the window of the airplane, with Robert P. Rabbit's face squeezed tightly between the two of them.

"Look!" said Katie. "Those are the biggest mountains I've ever seen."

"And they seem to go on forever," added Will. "I wonder if we are going to see them up close. I've never been in mountains like those. They are twice as big as the mountains in North Georgia."

"I think they are more than twice as big," said Robert P. Rabbit. "I had a cousin who used to live in those mountains, and he said that they are so high that trees can't even grow at the tops. And it looks like he was correct. I don't see any trees up at the very top of the highest ones. I wonder why. We'll have to ask someone when we get there."

Just then the flight attendant came by and told them to fasten their seat belts, as the plane was about to land. They craned their necks to look out of the window to see what the ground looked like as the plane came closer and closer. Katie said she thought she could see people now, and Will started waving just in case there was someone waving at us. He didn't want them to think we were rude by not waving back.

As the plane landed and taxied to the gate, we began to gather up all our stuff to be sure we didn't leave anything on the airplane. I didn't realize we had come on board with so much junk. There were books, magazines, bags of nuts, cookies, snacks, scarfs, coats, backpacks, water bottles, and even some binoculars that Will was using to see things on the ground as we flew over. Of course I was drafted to carry all of this off the plane, as everyone else was too busy watching how the ground came up so fast as we landed, and telling

Polly and everyone around us about the many things they had seen out the window.

After leaving the plane, we made our way to the baggage claim area and found the carousel where our bags would come in.

"How do they know which bags are ours?" asked Katie. "What if they get mixed up, and I end up with the bag of a really big lady? Nothing would fit me, and I wouldn't get to ski without my own ski suit."

"Don't worry," I said. "Our bags have tickets on them that match the tickets they gave Polly when she checked your bags in Atlanta. Besides, Polly put colored straps around all of our bags so they would not be confused with anyone else's bags. And Katie, I'll bet no one else coming into Denver has a bag like yours, with a picture of Rapunzel on it."

Sure enough, we got all our bags, and off we went to the car rental place. When we went out into the street, everyone finally found out what I had been telling them all along. Denver was COLD. About 30 degrees. I told them to be sure to put on their hats and gloves, because the wind chill factor would make it seem like it was 20 degrees.

"What's the wind chill factor, GrandDad?" asked Katie.

"Well," I said, "when the wind blows, the effect of the cold air against your skin is worse than if there is no wind at all because your body has a harder time heating your skin since all the heat you are creating is being blown away from your body by the wind, leaving your skin without the heat you are making."

Somehow I was not sure that all came out right, so I continued, "The harder the wind blows, the worse it is for your skin. In fact, if the temperature is below freezing, like it is now, the hard wind can give you frostbite really fast. That's why it is important to keep your skin covered up at all times."

"What's frostbite?" asked Will.

"It's something that happens to your fingers and toes when they become so cold that the blood stops flowing, and they freeze, just like things freeze in the fridge at home. Sometimes people lose their fingers and toes because of frostbite."

"GrandDad, stop saying things like that," said Polly. "You're going to scare the children."

"Yes, GrandDad," whimpered Katie. "I'm scared. I don't want to be here if I'm going to lose my fingers and toes. And what about my face? It's not covered up, and I don't want to lose my face."

"That's just great, GrandDad," said Polly. "How are you going to get out of this one?"

Thinking really fast, like they trained me to do in the Navy, I came up with a zinger that I hoped would calm everyone down. At least it did succeed in getting their minds off frostbite.

"Look," I yelled. "Here comes the car rental bus. Now we can all get on the bus and out of the wind. I don't see any frostbite on anyone, so I think we can safely say that Denver doesn't have any frostbite this year, so no one needs to worry. The bus is about to stop, so everyone grab your own suitcase so we can all get on the same bus. We don't want to leave anyone at the airport, now do we?"

So, for fear of being left at the airport, everyone dutifully pulled their suitcase closer to the curb and scrambled onto the bus as soon as the door opened. As the bus was pulling away from the curb, I heard Robert P. Rabbit telling Katie and Will that they didn't need to worry, rabbits don't get frostbite because of all their fur, and that if Katie or Will looked like they were getting frostbite he would cover their skin with his warm fur, and they wouldn't have to worry at all.

I winked at Robert P. Rabbit, and he rolled his eyes at me as if to say, "Aren't you glad I'm around to clean up all your messes?"

Because there were five of us—me, Polly, Wendy, Katie, and Will—well, really six with Robert P. Rabbit—and I didn't want to have to worry about the icy roads, I had rented a sturdy mountain SUV. We had about 130 miles to go, and there was no telling what the winter weather in the Rocky Mountains would be. With a stop for lunch, and multiple pit stops for the girls, it took us four hours to get to Avon.

"It should still be daylight when we get there since we gained two hours," I said.

"What do you mean we gained two hours?" asked Robert P. Rabbit.

"It's like this," I said. "Even though the flight was a three hour flight, and we left at 11:00 a.m., when we landed in Denver it was only noon instead of 2:00 p.m., like it was in Atlanta."

"That doesn't make sense," said Katie. "What happened to the other two hours? Did they just disappear, or did the clock move backward, or did we go through some kind of time warp like on *Star Trek*?"

"No," I answered. "The Earth is divided into time zones, and Atlanta is in the Eastern Time Zone. Where your cousin Emily lives in Mississippi, they are in the Central Time Zone. And where we are now, in the Rockies, we are in the Mountain Time Zone. Because the Earth is round, the sun doesn't rise at the same time all across the U.S. So when it rises in Atlanta at 6:00 a.m., it is another hour before it will rise in Mississippi. And since they want the sun to rise there at 6:00 a.m. too, they need for their clock to be one hour behind our clock in Atlanta. So when the sun rises in Atlanta at 6:00 a.m., it is still 5:00 a.m. in Mississippi. Then an hour later, when the sun rises in Mississippi, it will be 6:00 a.m. there. And by then in Atlanta it will be 7:00 a.m.. Does that make any sense, Katie?"

"Clear as mud," said Robert P. Rabbit.

Just then Polly said she was thirsty, and Will had to go to the bathroom, so I was saved from having to continue with the time problem, and I was certainly glad no one asked me about Daylight Savings time, which I'm not sure I understand myself. To distract everyone, all I had to do was mention Chick-fil-A and the brand new milkshakes they now serve, and immediately everyone's mind was off time and onto whether the vanilla or the peppermint milkshake was the best. Personally I like their lemon pie, and I had been eating as many of those as I could since I heard through the grapevine that they were going to stop selling them.

When we arrived in Avon, I showed everyone the neat traffic circles they have instead of stoplights. I told them how much better traffic moves through traffic circles than through a stoplight at an intersection.

"How do you know when you can get into the traffic circle, GrandDad?" asked Katie. "It looks like if everyone comes into the circle at the same time they would all run into each other."

"That's a good observation, Katie. The rule that keeps that from happening is that you always have to yield to the car on your left. If there is a car on your left, you have to let them go in front of you, and after they pass, you can then go out into the circle." By the time I had gone around the third circle, Katie and Will could both see how well it worked in keeping the traffic flowing.

In Avon, we were staying at the Westin Riverfront. It had a chairlift that came right into the hotel property, and that made it easy for Katie to get to the ski slopes, It also had a ski rental place, where we rented the special chair that Katie would use to ski.

"If I always have to be in a wheelchair, how can I ski?" she had asked. I told her to wait and see and it would be a surprise.

At the ski shop we were fitted for skis, boots and poles. But Katie's outfit was unique. First, she was fitted with boots, two-foot skis that fastened onto the boots, and poles that were were only about two-and-a-half-feet tall, with tiny little skis on the ends. And then there was the chair. The rest of us would ski standing up, but Katie would ski while sitting in a chair. The chair had runners just like skis, so that Katie would glide along the ground just like a sled being pulled by horses in the winter snow. In addition, as Katie would glide along the ground in her chair, her legs would be in front of her, and her little short skis would be going along the ground just like the skis on our feet would do. The poles would also glide along the ground right next to the runners on her chair. For Katie, the best part was that the chair had a basket in which she could put Robert P. Rabbit. Now he could enjoy the experience of skiing right alongside her.

"But GrandDad," she asked, "how do I steer myself, and how do I stop when I want to?"

"Well, Katie, that's the final piece of the puzzle. You can see that off the back of your chair is a strap—kind of like a water ski rope. I will ski behind you holding onto the rope, and when you need to slow down or stop, I will be able to do that for both of us. You can help steer by turning your skis one way or the other. When I see you turning, I will do the same, and I can help you turn by pulling on the side of the strap. You'll see, it works very well, and we should be able to keep up with everyone fairly easily. And we can get the chair up the mountain very easily, as they simply hook it onto the back of the ski lift chair we go up on."

That night was like the night before Christmas. It was very hard for everyone to get to sleep, since we were so anxious to go out on the slopes to start skiing. Katie, Robert P. Rabbit, and Will were up before everyone and kept coming into our room asking, "GrandDad, are you awake?" After about the third time I quit trying to fight it, so I got up to make breakfast. To give us energy, I made bacon, eggs, and pancakes, with lots of real maple syrup.

All the commotion woke up Polly and Wendy, so soon we were all dressed and headed to the ski and boot storage place. We put on our boots and grabbed our skis and poles. I picked up Katie's gear, and off we went to the chairlift. The ride to the base of the mountain in the chairlift was a new experience for all of them, and the buildings, trees, and slopes under us were covered with a white blanket of brand new snow. It truly was a winter wonderland like nothing they had ever seen in Atlanta, or even North Georgia. It was enough to amaze even Robert P. Rabbit, who was snuggled into Katie's backpack that she was now wearing on her front so she could carry him where she could see and talk to him.

The chairlift took us to Beaver Creek Mountain, where we bought our lift tickets and enrolled Will in his ski school. He had a wonderful teacher named Helga. His class consisted of eight boys, all about the same age, and they started their lesson on the beginner's slope. So Wendy and I could get some practice being behind Katie's chair, we started on the same beginner's slope as well. Everyone was doing so well that I knew we would all soon be going up the big mountain to the top of Beaver Creek.

The chairlifts to the top of the ski runs were hanging by cables that pulled us up the mountain. Sometimes we would be as high as a two-story house, and sometimes as high as a ten-story building. We sat with snow falling on us and our feet dangling down in space, sort of like a ride at Disney World or Six Flags.

Now we were at the top, and we had to make some choices. Beaver Creek Mountain has four levels of ski runs going down the mountain. First, there are Green runs that are not as steep, for beginning skiers and those who just wanted to relax and ski more slowly, enjoying the beautiful winter scenery. Then, there are Blue runs for intermediate skiers. These are the runs Polly, Wendy, and I used to take all the time, as we could go slow or fast, and they were a little more difficult than the Green runs.

The Black Diamond runs are for advanced skiers. These often had some severe bumps on them called moguls, and you didn't want to go down these runs unless you really knew what you were doing. And finally, the Black Double Diamond runs are for only the very best skiers, or the crazy teenagers who wanted to end up in a snow pile somewhere. While I've done a Black Diamond run from time to time in my younger days, I have never been foolish enough to try a Double Diamond.

We knew we would stick to the Green runs today. And

there were enough Green runs on the Beaver Creek Mountain to ski all day and almost never ski the same one twice.

After we had skied for the better part of the morning, we were all hungry and tired, so we skied down to the Spruce Saddle Lodge, where we could smell hamburgers cooking on the outdoor grill. Nothing tastes much better than a hamburger grilled over an open fire in the cold mountains of Colorado, especially if you have been skiing for three hours. Most people were eating out on the deck, so they watched as we skied up with Katie in her special chair with Robert P. Rabbit in her backpack in her lap. Katie was a big hit with the children. I suspect many of the grownups had the same questions the kids did, but were too embarrassed to ask.

"Is it hard to ski in a chair?" "Do you go very fast?" "What happens if your mother lets go of the strap? "Can you stop?" "Do you steer yourself?" "Do you ever get out of the chair to ski?"

Katie had a wonderful time answering all their questions and even offered to meet one girl at the top so they could ski down together.

A few mean people said she shouldn't be on the slopes because she probably slowed everyone else down. Of course this wasn't true, but these people were the kind who act out of ignorance rather than trying to find out the real truth. But Katie has gotten used to mean people, and she says she doesn't bother to get angry at them anymore; she just feels sorry for them for not trying to understand people who are different from them.

While we were eating, lo and behold, along came Will
and his whole class of eight boys. He saw Katie, and he was
very proud to be able to tell them that the girl they had all
seen skiing down the mountain in a chair was his sister. She
found herself answering all the same questions all over again,
but she didn't mind . When they finished eating, Will told us
that they were all headed to the top of the mountain for one
last run down to the Ski School. Wendy had to go down to
meet them when they got to the bottom, but Katie wanted to
try to follow them down.

"Oh GrandDad," she said. "Can we go up too and then
follow Will and his class all the way down?"

I wasn't sure that was such a good idea, as I didn't think
we could keep up. I had seen Will's class a couple of times already, and I could tell that they were all getting pretty good,
generally going a lot faster than I thought we should go. But
I agreed that we could try, so Katie and I went down to the
chair lift before Will and his group so we could be at the top
and be all ready to go down when they came up the chair
lift.

After we reached the top, we skied off to the side to wait
for Will. The run they were taking was called the Red Buffalo Run, and it went along the side of the ski property for
the first several hundred yards. While we were waiting, Katie
asked me about the red tape stretched between poles all along
the side of the run.

"That tape marks the edge of the ski boundary of the
Beaver Creek Mountain Resort. No one is allowed to go on

the other side of that red tape. It's out of bounds for all skiers, and you can get in trouble for crossing that boundary," I said. "Also, it is kind of a steep drop off on the other side of the tape, so it's not just out of bounds, it's unsafe as well."

"Why is there so much snow on the limbs of the trees over there?" asked Katie. "It looks like so much it would just break the limbs off."

"That's the way God made trees this high up where so much snow falls. As more and more snow gathers on the limbs, rather than breaking off, the limbs simply bend toward the ground. Eventually the snow slides off, and the limb springs back up again. Or if someone hits or shakes the tree, the snow will fall off as well."

By then Will and his class had gathered at the top and were starting to ski down. The instructor led the way while all eight boys followed exactly in her trail. She stopped every once in a while to be sure she had all her boys. As they started down, I heard a boy about their same age yell, "Dad, I'm going to follow these boys to the bottom."

"OK," said his dad. "I'll be a little ways behind you."

Katie and I took off behind Will's group down the Red Buffalo Run, but we soon lost them. It wasn't because Katie and I were going slow; we were skiing faster than we had all day. But Will and his group had gotten so good that they were skiing like intermediates—or even experts as far as I was concerned.

Once they had disappeared around the first big bend, we started skiing casually down Red Buffalo run. Once, I noticed Katie and Robert P. Rabbit talking to each other and pointing, but I wasn't about to try to stop to see what they were taking about. I was ready to get down and have some hot chocolate.

Little did I know that before the day was out, my little friends would turn into detectives and solve a mystery that no one else could solve.

CHAPTER EIGHT

KATIE AND ROBERT P. RABBIT: DETECTIVES IN THE MAKING

After a long run to the bottom of the slopes, we finally arrived at the Ski School area where there was a really big commotion going on. Groups of parents and kids stood around in small groups talking quietly among themselves. Ski Patrol workers wearing red jackets with a white cross on the back walked around asking the kids lots of questions. The Ski Patrol are like the police and firemen of the ski slopes. They help keep order on the slopes by not letting anyone go too fast or be reckless, and they are there when someone is injured or needs to be rescued. Once we saw a lady fall and hurt her leg, and the Ski Patrol came up the mountain in a snowmobile, wrapped her in blankets, put her on a sled that they towed behind the snowmobile, and took her down the slopes to be treated at the bottom.

When we saw Polly I asked her, "What's all the commotion about?"

She said, "When Will's ski class arrived at the Ski School, one of the boys who had been in the class was missing."

"How can that be?" I said. "Doesn't the instructor count her class each time they stop?"

"Yes, but a boy about the same size as all the others decided to join the line of kids and ski to the bottom with them. Somewhere before they stopped to rest the first time, the missing boy, Jeremy, left the group, so when the instructor counted her students, she had eight kids like she was supposed to have, and she just kept on going down the rest of the way with her class. Now they don't know where Jeremy is."

I remembered the boy and his father at the top of the ski lift when he asked his dad to let him follow the other boys to the bottom.

Not too far from where we were standing, Jeremy's parents were deep in conversation with the ski instructor and the Ski Patrol.

"Tell us what he was wearing," they said. "And give us a good description of what he looks like."

The parents gave the Ski Patrol detailed information so they could search the slopes for the missing boy. It was late in the afternoon, almost time for the upper lifts to be closed, so they planned to do a sweep of the slopes from the very top to the bottom in search of Jeremy. I could hear them radioing all of the lift operators to keep a lookout for Jeremy, in case he got on one of their lifts at any time. They were to stop him and immediately call the Ski Patrol office.

As we were standing there, one Ski Patrol officer asked Will if he remembered Jeremy.

"I sure do," said Will, "he was the fastest of us all, and he kept wanting to do lots of things the rest of us wouldn't do until we saw him do it. Like the time he went over a big bump and got air. After he did it we all did it, and it was great."

"Do you remember the last time you saw him?" he asked.

"Yeah," said Will. "At the top he was right behind me. We had waited to be the last ones in line so we could let the others get ahead a ways, and then we could go a lot faster than the group as we caught up. He was right behind me as we took off down the Red Buffalo Run. Then when we stopped for the first time, he wasn't there anymore."

"Why didn't you tell the instructor?" asked the Ski Patrolman.

"I was going to ask where he was, but just as I skied up we took off again, so I never had a chance to ask, and the instructor was so far ahead of me she wouldn't have heard me anyway."

"Maybe he is still on the Red Buffalo Run," I said.

"No," said the instructor. "We have already sent three Ski Patrolmen to come all the way down the runs the class took, including the Red Buffalo Run, and he isn't anywhere along that route that we can tell."

While all of this was going on, I could see Katie and Robert P. Rabbit deep in conversation. I asked them what they were talking about, wondering why they were concerned at all about Jeremy.

"We are certainly concerned," said Robert P. Rabbit, "and Katie and I think we know where he is."

"How do you think you know when the entire Beaver Creek Ski Patrol doesn't know, and you haven't even been on the mountain since he disappeared?" I said impatiently, thinking they really didn't seem to care about Jeremy at all.

"He's on the Red Buffalo Run, GrandDad," said Katie. "You need to go over and tell the Ski Patrol that they will find him up there."

"I've already suggested that to them, Katie, and they said they looked up there already and he's not there," I said.

"That's because they don't know where to look," said Robert P. Rabbit.

"Oh, and I suppose you know exactly where to look?" I said.

"Yes, I exactly do," said Robert P. Rabbit smugly.

"So why don't you let us all in on the little secret?" I said.

"Oh, stop it, you two. This isn't getting us anywhere. I think we should go right now to the top of the mountain, to the Red Buffalo Run, so we can show you where to find Jeremy. And we had better go quickly, as they said that they are going to close the lifts soon," said Katie.

"Why don't we just tell the Ski Patrol and let them go look?" I said.

"Because they won't believe me, and they won't try again. And we know they won't find him, and I heard one of them say that the temperature is going to drop to ten below zero tonight, and that if they don't find Jeremy, he will freeze to death. And we know they will be looking in all the wrong places. So please, GrandDad, we need to go up and find him right now."

I told Polly and Wendy that Katie and I were going to the top of the mountain because we thought we knew where to find Jeremy, and we would be down as soon as we could. After I explained it all to Polly, she said she agreed one hundred per cent with Katie, which made Katie grin ear to ear, and we took off as fast as we could.

We first took the Centennial Express quad lift. It holds four people, and we thought we might need Will to help us, so he got on with us. We had to ski down from one lift to another, but after taking the Cinch Express lift, we found ourselves at the top of the Red Buffalo Run just as they were shutting that lift down, making us almost the last people at the top of the mountain.

On the way up, Katie and Robert P. Rabbit explained their theory about where we would find Jeremy.

"Its like this, GrandDad," said Katie. "Do you remember when we were at the top and we saw all of Will's class come off the lift and start down?"

"Yes," I said. "We followed them to see how good Will was doing."

"Well after we lost them so quickly, because they were going so fast, you showed us the red tape that marked the edge of the Ski Resort Boundary. And you said that no one was allowed to go beyond that tape, and that if they did, it was a pretty steep drop-off on the other side of it."

"I remember," I said.

"When we get to the top, we need to go down right next to the red tape, and we need to look for something Robert P. Rabbit and I saw as we were coming down. First, look closely at the fir trees. They are all covered with deep snow, and they all look like big Christmas trees that have a layer of snow on each branch. You told us how God made these trees to hold snow, remember? Robert P. Rabbit and I remembered how we all got under one of these trees back at the condo, and how you shook the trunk and we all got totally covered with snow. So as we were coming down Red Buffalo Run, we started looking at the trees on the other side of the boundary to see which tree we would want to stand under when the snow came down."

"OK," I said, "but what does that have to do with Jeremy?"

"As we were coming down the slope," said Robert P. Rabbit, "we saw one tree where there wasn't much snow at all on the branches. And we saw tracks of a skier who obviously had gone off the run, under the red tape, and had hit the tree. It was the only tree anywhere around that didn't have any snow on it. At the time we thought it was funny, and we would have liked to see the skier after he climbed back onto Red Buffalo Run. But now we realize it must be Jeremy."

Wow, this all made such good sense. I was very sure that they were right and that we needed to get to Jeremy as soon as we could. He had been missing for at least two hours, and he must be very cold.

At the top I told Will to lead the way and to not go too fast so we wouldn't miss the tracks of Jeremy's skis where they went under the boundary.

We found that in several places there were other runs that either joined or left Red Buffalo. First we passed Jack Rabbit Alley, which really interested Robert P. Rabbit, as he thought he might find some cousins down that run, and then we got to the junction of Cinch Road and the Stone Creek Chutes. But Will knew just where to turn so we would stay on Red Buffalo.

Finally, after making it down the run about halfway, Katie cried out, "There they are, GrandDad." And sure enough, off to our right, going right under the red tape, were the tracks of two skis. There was a sharp drop-off, and the tracks were so shallow that the ski patrol would never have noticed them.

We all stopped and looked down the steep slope. Sure enough, about twenty feet down the slope, the tracks stopped right at the trunk of a big fir tree. We couldn't tell if anyone was at the base of the tree, because just as Katie and Robert P. Rabbit had said, all of the snow had fallen off the branches and had covered anything that was at the base of the tree.

"We've got to get down there right away," I said.

"Wait right here," said Robert P. Rabbit. "This world of snow is my world, not yours. My feet are made for going through the snow without sinking in, so let me go look."

With that Robert P. Rabbit leaped out of Katie's lap and down into the snow under the big fir tree.

"He's here!" yelled Robert P. Rabbit. "And he is very cold, so I am going to crawl into his jacket to help keep him warm while you come down to get him."

"I'll help you," said Will.

"NO!" I said. "Will, you are the fastest skier, and someone needs to ski down to the beginning of the Drink of Water Lift and tell the lift operator that we have found Jeremy, and they need to get up here right away. Do you think you can do that all alone?" I asked.

"I can do it, GrandDad. I remember the run really well, and I know just where we got on that lift," said Will. And off he went as fast as I had seen him ski all day.

I unfastened the bindings of my skis so I could walk down to the tree, leaving Katie in her chair to wave down anyone who might come by. But because we were the last ones up this lift, I didn't think anyone would be coming soon enough to help Jeremy, so it looked like we needed to do something ourselves right away.

When Robert P. Rabbit had gone down to Jeremy, he only sank a few inches into the snow. I was sinking down to my waist with each step, and I then knew what Robert P. Rabbit meant when he said this was "his world." It was quite a struggle, but I soon made it all the way down to the base of the tree, and there I found Jeremy. I knew he was not too seriously hurt because he was crying, and the snow covering him and his ski jacket had kept him from getting frostbite, but I was sure that hypothermia might be setting in if we didn't get him warm as soon as possible. I could tell by the trampled snow that he had tried to get out, but the snow was just too deep, and one of his skis had become wedged between a tree and a big rock, so he couldn't get it off. When I reached him, I reassured him that we were going to get him out. I could tell by his words and movements that his back was not injured, which was a relief to me.

On my way down I had acted like a human snow plow, pushing the snow out of the way and tramping it down so it would be easier coming out. So after I had released Jeremy's foot from the stuck ski, I picked him up and worked my way back up the hill to where Katie was waiting in her chair.

"GrandDad, put him in the chair with me, and give me your ski jacket so we can wrap him up some more. And take off his ski boots and wrap his feet in your ski hat and scarf to help warm them up," she said.

So I did what I was told, and before long Katie, Robert P. Rabbit, and Jeremy were all snug and cozy in Katie's ski chair, while I was left standing there with no hat, no scarf, and no jacket. But that was OK. I figured I wouldn't have to shiver too long if Will skied as fast as I thought he could.

But then I remembered that the Drink Of Water ski lift had a warming hut for the staff, and since the Ski Patrol would have to come right by it to get to us, I decided to start down with them all in Katie's chair. If the Ski Patrol didn't get here right away, we could all wait for them in the warming hut. Just as we reached the hut, we saw three snowmobiles racing up Cinch Road with their red and blue lights flashing like crazy. Each snowmobile was pulling a sled, and on each sled was a red clad Ski Patrol officer with a white cross on their back. I knew now that Jeremy would be safe.

They immediately loaded Jeremy into one of the sleds, and Katie with Robert P. Rabbit into another, and down the mountain they flew. I breathed a sigh of relief and was just about to go out of the warming hut to put my skis back on and ski down to the bottom, when a rather strong-looking Ski Patrol lady came up to me and said, "OK, now it's your turn. I'm going to prepare you for the trip down so we can get you to a warm, safe place."

"You don't need to do that," I said. "I'm already in a warm and safe place; and I can ski down on my own."

"Don't give me any problems," she said. "Just do what I say."

"But I'm not hurt," I said.

"You will be if you don't follow instructions," she said. "Once you call us for help, and we send the snowmobiles up, we are in charge, and we decide who needs help and who doesn't. And I've decided that you need help. So do what I say."

By this time I was convinced that she must be a martial arts instructor and that it would be best if I didn't argue with her anymore. Besides, Katie still had my ski jacket and hat, and it was getting colder every minute, so a ride down covered in a warm blanket didn't seem like a bad idea after all. So I put on the jump suit she provided, wrapped myself in a warm blanket and lay down on the sled. She strapped me in a little tighter than I thought she needed to, and off we went down the mountain. I think she was trying to prove to me all over again who was in charge as she sped down the mountain, I'm certain hitting many more bumps than she needed to, and taking curves so fast the sled almost turned on its side.

When we got down, I thanked her profusely, apologized for any trouble I had caused, and told her I appreciated that she thought of my safety first by not letting me ski down the mountain with no hat or jacket. I could tell that softened her up, and she even gave me a little hug when we parted.

Polly then came up and said that Jeremy's parents wanted to see me, so we went into the Ski School where they were waiting. Jeremy had been taken into a room where the doctor was making sure he was OK.

As soon as they saw us they ran up and hugged me. They were crying tears of happiness. I was a little embarrassed, and I told them so.

"It wasn't me," I said, "It was Katie and Robert P. Rabbit."

"Who's Robert P. Rabbit?" they said.

Not knowing exactly what to say, I simply said, "Oh, he's my granddaughter's pet rabbit." I quickly changed that subject and went on to tell them, and the Ski Patrol people who were standing nearby, how Katie, on her own, had solved the mystery. I assured them that I was skeptical, and thus didn't come right to a Ski Patrol officer as I had been told that the Red Buffalo Run had already been searched. I'm not sure I should have said that, as one of the Ski Patrol winced when I said it, but it didn't matter as the parents were so fascinated with the fact that Katie had been smart enough to figure out what had happened to Jeremy, that that was all they wanted to talk about for the next ten minutes. They were very anxious to thank her in person, which they did when Katie came out of the doctor's room, where they had been talking to her.

As we all got into the car to go back to the condo, Katie couldn't stop talking.

"GrandDad," she said, "they were so nice to me. They said we all can ski the rest of the time we are here for free. And they gave me coupons so we can eat all we want on the slopes at no charge. And they are going to give Will private lessons every day. And they gave me this big bag of chocolate chip cookies. And best of all they have made me an honorary member of the Beaver Creek Mountain Ski Patrol, and they gave me a patch to prove it that Polly can sew onto the sleeve of my ski jacket. Oh GrandDad, don't you just love it here?"

The rest of our ski trip was the best ever. We skied every day, and when we came to a lift or to a group of Ski Patrol, they would clap for Katie as if she were a big celebrity. We ate so many hamburgers at the Spruce Saddle restaurant on the slopes I thought I would never want one again. Will was an excellent skier by the end of the trip and was even going down the expert slopes. He said next time he wanted to snowboard rather than ski.

And as for Robert P. Rabbit, he made sure I knew that if it weren't for him being so insistent with me, they would never have found Jeremy in time.

And he was right, and I told him so.

CHAPTER NINE

THE GREAT EASTER EGG HUNT

After we came home from Avon, it was spring holidays. All the children were out of school for a week and a half, and that meant Katie's cousins, Emily and Mary Brooks, were coming to visit from Mississippi. Katie had always lived in the same house, in the same town, all of her life—Tallulah Falls, Georgia, population 160—except when Katie and her family came to stay with us in Atlanta, then the population dipped to 154. But Emily and Mary Brooks's father was a Marine, and so they had lived in some exotic places like Quantico, Virginia; Cherry Point, North Carolina; and even New Orleans, Louisiana. But now they were in Atlanta at our house, and the big event everyone was looking forward to was the annual Easter egg hunt at Stone Mountain, Georgia. On this day, thousands of eggs are hidden all over a big field at the base of the largest outcropping of granite in the United States, and hundreds of kids are turned loose to run as fast as they can, carrying a basket to fill with eggs. In addition to the eggs, each child is given a soft, cuddly, stuffed rabbit.

Why there are always rabbits at Easter, along with chicken eggs, is a mystery to me, but Robert P. Rabbit was more than happy to explain.

"Look, big boy," he said, "chickens are basically ugly creatures. They have short, spindly legs, funny looking wings they never use to fly, rather pointed and ugly beaks, and they walk around eating disgusting bugs all day. Besides, what most people know most about chickens is that you find them at Chick-fil-A battered and fried in grease, made into little nuggets, and served in little boxes with ketchup.

"And besides," he said, "how many kids do you know who want to curl up in bed at night with a chicken?"

I couldn't think of anyone I knew who slept with a chicken, so I said nothing.

"On the other hand," he said, "what a joy to every child lucky enough to have a soft, cuddly bunny rabbit to snuggle up to when the bedroom lights go out, and the kid needs to be comforted in the dark, because Mommy and Daddy have abandoned the poor child so they can go watch another boring TV show."

He made his point, so I told him so. We had a bigger problem. Katie had recently received treatment that made her a little unstable on her feet when she tried to walk on her own, so we had to make sure she stayed in her wheelchair. This meant that she couldn't run out onto the field with the other children but would have to stay on the concrete walkway where she would be able to push herself along, or someone else could push her. The chances of her finding any eggs on the side of the walkway, I said, especially the gold plastic ones with the Susan B. Anthony gold dollars in them, were slim to none.

"Don't worry," said Robert P. Rabbit, "I can solve that problem. Just take me to the field about an hour before the hunt starts, and I'll do some magic with the hidden eggs."

I wasn't sure what he meant by "magic," but I didn't know what else to do, so off we went an hour before the hunt was to start. Besides, I had long since ceased questioning Robert P. Rabbit when he had a plan.

When we got to Stone Mountain, Katie, Emily, Mary Brooks, and their parents went to the playground to swing and play, and I took Robert P. Rabbit to the field where the eggs were hidden.

"Put me down here," he said.

"But there is a ribbon around the field to keep people off until the hunt starts," I said.

He said, "Ribbons don't count against rabbits," and off he hopped under the ribbon and out into the field.

I looked around to see if any of the officials guarding the field were going to come arrest us, but they just pointed to this cute little bunny rabbit hopping all over the field as if he were just a natural thing to expect on this fine Easter morning. After watching him and laughing at him for awhile, they turned back to guarding the ribbon and simply ignored him. I could see him hopping about the concrete sidewalk that wound through the field and along which we would have to take Katie, and soon he came hopping back and jumped up into my arms.

"Okay, big boy, it's all ready."

I wasn't sure just what he meant by "all ready," but I didn't think I wanted to know. So back we went to the playground to gather up our crew and to return to the ribbon to wait for the signal that the Great Stone Mountain Easter Egg Hunt was underway.

At 10:00 a.m. sharp, the horns sounded, the ribbon was cut, and hundreds of kids went running onto the field to find eggs, Emily and Mary Brooks included. Katie and two other girls and one boy, who were also in wheelchairs, had to enter the field on the walkway and try to find any eggs that were close enough to reach along the walkway. All four of us pushers could see that so many kids were running along ahead of us, that in just minutes every egg that was anywhere near the pathway was grabbed up and put into someone else's basket. Robert P. Rabbit could see that I was very disappointed. Whatever he had done just didn't work.

Emily and Mary Brooks came back and offered to get some eggs for Katie, but Katie just smiled and told them not to worry, she would find plenty of eggs. She winked at Robert P. Rabbit and he winked back at her with his one pink eye, the only one he used to wink at Katie. When he winked at me, he always used his blue eye, saving his pink one for special occasions with special people.

Katie asked us to let the four of them in wheelchairs be allowed to face each other and talk. So we let them do it. We
couldn't hear what Katie was telling the other three, but it
must have been good as they all giggled and smiled, and then
we placed them in a little row one behind the other as we
were instructed by Katie, with Katie and Robert P. Rabbit in
her lap bringing up the rear.

As we began to push them down the path, Robert P. Rabbit would tell Katie something, and Katie would yell out to
one of the other kids in front of her where to look for an egg.

"Stop and look under that little pile of sticks," she would
say, or "Look under that rock by the post," or "Look in that
old can lying there," or "Look in that paper bag over there."

This went on for half an hour until each child had at least
a dozen eggs in their basket. All of the eggs had been hidden
from the other children and thus had not been taken yet. The
four children were very happy. While Robert P. Rabbit was
out in the field before the hunt had started, he had hidden at
least three dozen eggs where none of the other children who
were running around so fast would see them. They were all
just looking for eggs that were in plain sight, where almost
all of them were, since the grownups had merely scattered
a couple thousand eggs over the top of the field, not taking
the time to hide them particularly well. Only the eggs that
Robert P. Rabbit hid were actually out of sight, and so they
were the ones that the children in the wheelchairs were able
to find.

By the time the hunt was over, Emily and Mary Brooks came running back with their baskets full of beautifully colored eggs, many of which were filled with delicious candy (they were plastic eggs, of course), and as they showed their treasures to Katie, it suddenly occurred to me that there were no eggs in Katie's basket at all. In all the excitement, I had not noticed that Katie had told the other children where eggs were hidden, but she had not asked for any of them for herself.

"Katie," I said, "why didn't you tell me to get some of the eggs for you?"

"Oh GrandDad," she said, "I wanted the other children to have full baskets of eggs. I didn't really need any."

"But Katie," I said, "we want you to have some eggs."

"Don't worry, GrandDad, Emily is going to help me find some eggs that none of the other children have found yet." And Emily immediately took command of the situation by pushing Katie's wheelchair as we started back toward the parking lot. As they went along, I could see Robert P. Rabbit whisper something to Katie, Emily, or Mary Brooks, and they would dart away and come back with two or three eggs for Katie's basket. By the time we got back to the car, Katie had at least twenty eggs in her basket. She even had three big golden eggs with a fine Susan B. Anthony dollar in each for herself, Emily, and Mary Brooks.

Suddenly I realized that Robert P. Rabbit had been talking directly to Emily and Mary Brooks, so I asked him about that.

"They have THE MARK," he said, "and I have been talking to them ever since they arrived."

What a pleasant surprise this was. Now I didn't have to hide from them that I was talking to a rabbit.

After we left the park, Katie, Emily, and Mary Brooks spent all the way home in the van laughing and giggling, opening up their eggs and eating a ton of jellybeans and chocolate candy, and all the time Robert P. Rabbit was curled up in Katie's lap asleep. He had put in quite a long day already, and was obviously quite tired.

CHAPTER TEN

RADIATION DAY

It was early in the morning, and we were still in bed at that time when you aren't sure whether you are awake or asleep, when I sensed that someone else was in the room besides just Polly and me. So I opened my eyes while lying on my side, and sure enough, a few inches from my face were the sweet, smiling eyes of Katie.

"Get up, GrandDad," she said. "It's Friday, and I get to go to radiation treatment today."

"Okay, Katie, but just give me another minute or two to wake up," I said.

"Lift me up in the bed, GrandDad, and I'll help you wake up," she said.

So I reached down and pulled her up into the bed so she could lie between Polly and me as she had done so many times before. Immediately she began to sing one of her favorite morning songs:

Wakey, wakey, rise and shine
You've had your sleep, I've had mine
Get up, get up, sleepy head
Get up, get up, out of bed

Before she could sing the second verse, up into the bed popped Robert P. Rabbit, right onto my stomach.

He wasn't sure exactly what all the excitement was all about, so he turned to Katie and said, "Katie, why are you so excited about going to radiation treatment?"

Katie said, "The radiation doctor says he thinks the treatments might help heal me, and I think that is really exciting."

"Well, that's good enough for me. When we do go?" said Robert P. Rabbit.

"As soon as we can get GrandDad out of bed," she said.

"Okay," said Robert P. Rabbit. "I can accomplish that. Just give me a few minutes and watch what I do." This was usually a sign that something was about to happen that might not be the best for me.

With that, Robert P. Rabbit bounced off the bed at the same time that Polly said with a sleepy voice, "What's going on, Katie? You seem to be answering questions that no one is asking."

Knowing that Polly couldn't hear Robert P. Rabbit, Katie

thought quickly of a response. "That's okay, Polly," said Katie. "I'm just making it easy for GrandDad. He's so sleepy that I didn't want him to have to ask questions, so I'm answering the questions before he asks them."

Polly looked sort of confused and rolled over on the bed to try to go back to sleep. Before anyone else could say a thing, up on the bed came Pepper, running around in circles as if she were chasing her own tail, first on Polly, then on Katie, then on me, and then on Katie again. Up came Robert P. Rabbit following Pepper, nipping at her tail. Both of them were all over the bed playing a very excited and rambunctious game of tag. Katie shrieked with joy, and it was almost impossible for me to stay in bed, and Polly certainly couldn't stay there with all the commotion.

Robert P. Rabbit's plan had worked, because I got up, showered, and shaved, and Polly helped Katie get dressed, and down to the car we all went. There was no breakfast on radiation day, but we did have some juice and spent part of the time on the way to the hospital planning what we would have to eat when we finally could have breakfast after the treatment.

"I want two cinnamon donuts, a peanut butter roll-up, some raspberries, and an apple juice," said Katie.

"I want bacon, eggs, grits, toast, and coffee," I said.

"I guess I'll have some carrots," said Robert P. Rabbit, without enthusiasm.

"Is that all you want? It sure doesn't sound like much," said Katie.

"Well," said Robert P. Rabbit, "if you must know, I'd really like to have a rutabaga, but no one ever gives us rabbits rutabagas. We always get carrots, lettuce, and occasionally a bit of cabbage. But no one ever gives us a rutabaga, probably because they don't really know what they are."

"Wow," said Katie. "We'll have to find you a rutabaga today, won't we, GrandDad?"

"I guess so," I said, even though Robert P. Rabbit was right. I wasn't sure I would know a rutabaga when I saw one.

Just then we arrived at the hospital. Katie turned to Robert P. Rabbit and said, "Watch this, Robert P. Rabbit. GrandDad says I am so important here that I get to go right into the emergency area and park in one of the special spaces. Not everyone gets to do that, but because I get radiation treatment, we get this special privilege." With that, we pulled into one of the handicapped places, and I got Katie's wheelchair out of the back of the car. She didn't have to use the wheelchair all of the time, but when we were at the hospital they wanted her to use it. By the time we got into the door, Robert P. Rabbit had made himself inanimate while in Katie's lap so they would let him in, and we went straight to Radiology, where Katie would get her radiation treatment.

First, we went to the receptionist's desk to sign in.

"Hello, Mrs. Wilson," said Katie. "I brought two tomatoes for you from my grandmother's garden. She said they are organic, which means they won't hurt you with the poison that some farmers put on their tomatoes to kill bugs."

"Thank you very much," said Mrs. Wilson. "I'll put them on my sandwiches for lunch."

Then we went to the nurse's station where Katie saw her friend, Ms. Stephens.

"Hello, Ms. Stephens, I brought you some daisies from our front yard. If you put a little sugar in the water with the daisies they will last a lot longer," she said.

"Thank you, Katie, they will certainly brighten up my day," she said.

From the first day we had started going to radiation, Katie had made friends with the people there. It always seemed to brighten their day when Katie arrived, as she always had a nice word for them and usually remembered to bring gifts of some sort.

While we waited for Katie's turn, little Stanley came out of the treatment room, and Ms. Agnes, who must have been at least eighty years old, came in through the receptionist area. Katie knew them both very well, as they had been together in the treatment center many times. She introduced them to Robert P. Rabbit, and she spent at least ten minutes telling them all of the wonderful things that Robert P. Rabbit could do.

When Katie's turn came, she asked if Robert P. Rabbit could go into the room with her. The doctor said that while the radiation was good for her, it might hurt Robert P. Rabbit, so he could not go into the room with her. So while Katie went in, I held Robert P. Rabbit on my lap.

"How long does it take?" he asked me.

"About twenty minutes," I said.

"What do they do?" he continued.

"Well, they have her lie down on a table, and they put this fancy device on her head. Then they put her into a very large machine, and they direct a radiation beam at the cancer in her head in hopes of destroying it."

We didn't talk anymore until Katie came out, as everyone in the waiting room was wondering why I was talking to a stuffed animal.

When Katie came out and we returned to the car, Robert P. Rabbit asked her about what it was like in the treatment room. She told him all about it—especially about the big machine that was like a giant rocket ship. She said that she just closed her eyes and dreamed that she was an astronaut and that all the devices they put on her were part of her space helmet and space suit, and the big tube she went into was going to take her to the moon. Then she would imagine that she was taking off from the Earth on her way into space. It was quite fascinating listening to how Katie's imagination had helped her so much in handling the treatment room all by herself.

As we drove along, I was lost in her conversation, and she suddenly looked over at me and shouted, "GrandDad, turn around! You just passed Whole Foods. We have to go get Robert P. Rabbit a rutabaga."

"Hey," said Robert P. Rabbit, "that sounds like a great idea to me."

So I did a U-turn and into the parking lot we went. As I was getting Katie's wheelchair out, without warning, Robert P. Rabbit bounded out of the car and hopped straight into the grocery store, all excited about perhaps finally finding a rutabaga. I knew that was not going to be good, so we hurried after him as fast as we could.

As it turned out, he made it past the checkout counter without being seen, but as he went down the first aisle searching for the vegetables, he was spotted by a teenage grocery clerk, who immediately went after him. As might be expected with a teenage boy, catching the rabbit was more important than using care not to knock anything off the shelves. The first thing to go was a stack of ketchup bottles that had been put out into the aisle for a special sale. At least a dozen broke when they hit the floor, spilling ketchup everywhere. Next was the stack of drink cans at the end of the aisle that went rolling in every direction.

The commotion caused two ladies, running in opposite directions, to collide by the table of apples, not only sending the contents of their baskets all over the floor, but also dumping the apples into the next aisle, where two seven-year-old boys decided to use the apples as missiles to launch over the tops of the aisles to see how many other aisles they could reach with a good pitch. Just then I caught up with Robert P. Rabbit and put him in Katie's lap, and he immediately came to his senses and took on his best "stuffed rabbit" look.

By then the teenage grocery clerk was collared by his boss, and as we hurried to the produce section, we heard the boy trying to explain about a rabbit on the loose in the store. The boss replied in a very upset tone that the only rabbit in the store was a stuffed rabbit, and that it was in the lap of a little girl in a wheelchair, and that it could not possibly have caused all of this damage. The poor teenage grocery clerk looked very confused, but we didn't say anything as we went on to the vegetable department, as I knew there was no way we could make anyone understand what had just happened.

When we finally got back home and Katie was eating her special breakfast, I tried to tell Polly all that had happened, but I didn't know where to start, and it didn't come out right, and Polly just looked at me like I had gone crazy. And all Robert P. Rabbit did was to wink at me with his blue eye and keep eating away at his very special rutabaga.

Well, at least from now on I know what a rutabaga looks like.

CHAPTER ELEVEN

WHOSE IDEA WAS IT, ANYWAY?

It was always easier for Katie to go through her treatments if Emily was visiting. How nice it is to have a best friend to sleep with you and talk with you and hug you when you need it. That is what Emily did for Katie. Since Emily's dad was a Marine, he was often deployed overseas, and this spring he was in Iraq. To make things easier for our other daughter, Jenna, and so Emily and Katie could be together, Emily came to live with us until her father came home. It was a joy for Katie to find out that Emily too had THE MARK, so Emily fit right into the adventures with Robert P. Rabbit.

Also, when they were together, Katie, Emily, and Robert P. Rabbit spent many hours plotting and planning the next great events for our family. One of their favorite pastimes was to sit in a circle on the floor with Katie and Emily and Robert P. Rabbit first talking, then whispering, then bursting out in laughter and falling back on the floor in great delight as they thought of their ideas.

Some afternoons they would play dress-up with the wonderful, bright, and fancy clothes that Polly kept in a large flower-painted chest in the playroom. Emily was always the queen with a tiara and a wand with a star on the end of it. Katie was always the princess dressed in a silver dress with a white boa and sparkly slippers. Robert P. Rabbit was always the handsome prince with a sash around his waist into which they put a small plastic knife that served as his sword.

But when summer came and the time drew near when Emily might have to go back to Mississippi, the three of them began planning just what they could do to solve the problem of not wanting to be apart. They thought everyone should know by now that it would be much better if they were all three together as much as possible, especially for the long summer months. To this task, Robert P. Rabbit began to put forth his best efforts, and came up with a very good plan. Unbeknownst to me, this plan required me to be the main character, making a decision that at the time seemed like my idea. Looking back now, I see I was just a pawn in the game. Before I even knew it, the outcome had been well thought out by the Queen, the Princess, and most of all, the handsome Prince, Robert P. Rabbit.

To appreciate the plan you have to understand that where Katie lives in Tallulah Falls, Georgia, there is no cable TV. The town is at the base of the Appalachian Mountains, and the powers that be in the TV world just have not deemed it profitable to run a cable all the way up to Tallulah Falls for 160 people. And the satellite dish doesn't get good reception because of the mountains and the trees surrounding Katie's little mountain house. So for entertainment, Katie's parents have always bought old TV shows at flea markets and showed them on the VHS or DVD. Thus, Katie grew up watching reruns of *Little House on the Prairie, Bonanza, I Love Lucy,* and her absolute favorite, *Gilligan's Island. Gilligan's Island* was about a group of very funny people that were shipwrecked and stranded on a tropical island in the middle of the ocean, an island with palm trees, coconuts, sand, starfish, seashells, and lots of bright sunshine.

So in early June, the three of them began dropping subtle hints. Robert P. Rabbit said to me one day, "Hey, big boy, do you happen to have a beach towel I can borrow?"

"Why sure," I said, and I got him my favorite blue beach towel with a fish on it that looks like Nemo. "What do you want it for?" I said.

"I'm going to put it on the little bed you made for me and sleep on it." Later he asked me, "Do you have some beach chairs we can use?"

"I think so," I said, and I went to the garage and found three small beach chairs just their size. "What do you want with these?" I asked.

"Well, we just thought it would be nice to eat our meals sitting in beach chairs," he said.

And from then on when the girls would have their sandwiches and Kool-Aid for lunch, and Robert P. Rabbit his rutabaga, they would eat lounging back in their beach chairs with their towels behind their heads just as comfortable as you please. It all seemed out of place to me seeing them like this at most every meal, with sunglasses on to boot, but soon

it really got out of hand. The girls started wearing their bathing suits around all day long instead of their play clothes.

"What's going on?" I asked Polly.

"I think they are trying to tell you something," she said.

For the life of me, I couldn't figure that one out, and Polly was no help at all. She just rolled her eyes as if to say, "If you don't know, I'm not going to be the one to tell you."

One day we were in the middle of a real heat wave in Atlanta. The temperature reached in the upper 90s, the sun was at its highest, and we hadn't had rain in weeks.

"What do you do around here to stay cool, big boy?" said Robert P. Rabbit.

"You stay inside where it is air conditioned," I said.

"What if you want to go outside?" he said.

"Well, you can wait until the sun goes down and its cooler," I said, proud of myself for having been able to give him such an answer.

Robert P. Rabbit seemed to think about that one for a minute, and then he said, "But that won't do if you want to play catch, or tag, or hide-n-seek, or throw a ball or a Frisbee. It would be just too dark outside. I would think that a man as smart as you are supposed to be could do better than that."

I took that as a definite challenge, so I really put my thinking cap on and came up with a zinger. "The best way to cool off is to go to the beach and take a dip in the ocean," I said, feeling very proud of myself for thinking of such a grand solution.

"Tell me about the beach and the ocean," he said.

"You mean you've never been to the beach?" I asked.

"Of course not, I'm a mountain rabbit. Coming to Atlanta was my first time out of the North Georgia mountains."

So I called Katie in to tell Robert P. Rabbit about the beach. He listened intently to everything she said, but had the most questions about the soft sand that went on for miles each way, and the waves that came in from the ocean and broke on the sand. Robert P. Rabbit had seen a lake before, but it didn't have waves, and you could see to the other side. Katie told him that at the ocean you can't see the other side because it is so big, and for Robert P. Rabbit this was hard to imagine.

Then Katie started talking about *Gilligan's Island*. She was sure they filmed the show just to the south of Atlanta at a place we sometimes visited in South Carolina called Hilton Head Island.

I tried to think of the first time I had been to the ocean. I was twelve years old at the time. How exciting it was to see palm trees with coconuts growing on them. And the crabs running along the sand in front of the incoming waves was fascinating. Also finding starfish and conch shells every time the tide went out was something that kept me busy every afternoon. But most of all, the cool ocean breeze and the refreshing water was what I remembered.

"Hey," I said, "do you all want to go to the beach to cool off?"

"And maybe we can find where they filmed *Gilligan's Island!*" said Katie, who almost shouted in excitement. "And we can bring Emily and her family and my family and Polly and have such a grand time."

And before I knew it Katie was off to tell Emily and Polly that we were all going to the beach, and everyone was coming with us, and we were going to stay at least two weeks, and we could swim in the ocean every day and find seashells and build sandcastles, and it would be the best beach trip ever

because it would be Robert P. Rabbit's first time to see the
ocean.

When I followed Katie into the kitchen where Polly and Emily were making cookies, Polly just looked at me
and smiled. Then later, Robert P. Rabbit said to me, "Well
big boy, sometimes you do come up with some pretty good
ideas."

For some reason I just didn't feel like it was entirely my
idea. But then it really didn't matter whose idea it was in
the first place, because when you are thinking about how
to please someone else, you have to know what they really
want, and not what you want that you hope they will like,
and this decision obviously pleased everyone immensely.

CHAPTER TWELVE

KATIE DOES HER PART

The trip from Atlanta to Hilton Head Island was a little more complicated than we had planned on. First, because there were so many of us, we needed to take Wendy and Carl's mini-van as well as my SUV. Katie and Robert P. Rabbit wanted to ride with me, and Polly wanted to ride with the boys in the other car. So I needed Arielle, who was fifteen, in my car to help me with Katie if Katie needed anything while I was driving.

We also had the wheelchair with us in case Katie needed to get out of the car and go to the ladies' room at a rest stop. We drove together with one car in front of the other, and with so many in our group, more pit stops than normal were necessary.

For Robert P. Rabbit, it was his first time to be in a car for any distance since he had come to Atlanta in the back of a pick-up truck, which is another story altogether. He was full of questions that Katie and I tried to answer as best we could. Arielle tolerated Katie and I talking to a rabbit as if it were just as normal as anything. (Keep in mind that Arielle does not have THE MARK.) Of course, it helped a lot that as a teenager who was being forced to leave her friends for two long weeks, Arielle spent most of her time texting on her cell phone with her earplugs firmly in place. Thus she didn't really hear us talking at all anyway and paid very little attention to anything going on around her. As for Robert P. Rabbit, he was full of his usual questions whenever he encountered anything new to him.

"Why is everyone going so fast on this highway?" asked Robert P. Rabbit, as we headed down I-75 out of Atlanta.

"This highway has only limited access for cars coming on from the other roads," I said. "So with only a few places for other cars to enter the highway, we can all go faster than normal."

"That doesn't tell me why we all go so fast," he said. "What is the big hurry?"

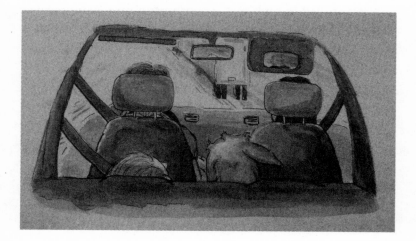

"Well," I said, "I guess it's because we would rather be where we are going to end up than on this highway, so we want to get there as fast as we can."

"You don't say," he said. "Is everyone going where we are going?" he asked.

"No," I said. "We are all going different places."

"Then why are we all on the same road?" he asked.

"Well this road goes to lots and lots of towns and cities, so whenever someone gets to where they want to go, they simply get off this road and the rest of us keep on going."

"You don't say," he said. "How will we know when we get to where we want to get off?" he asked.

"Well," I said, "there will be a sign that tells us that to get to Hilton Head Island we will need to get off the highway."

"You don't say," he said. "Why are there so many signs on the side of the highway?" he asked.

These questions went on and on for hours until he didn't have any more questions to ask and had finally fallen asleep in Katie's lap. Katie had fallen asleep long ago, having gotten bored with all of Robert P. Rabbit's questions. And Arielle was still busy texting her friends, telling them how she was sure her GrandDad had totally lost it as he had just spent almost the entire trip talking to a rabbit.

Just as things had calmed down and I was looking forward to some peace and quiet, I looked ahead on the highway and saw the back of a big tractor trailer truck swerve to the left and into the path of the other lanes of traffic. The driver had either fallen asleep or just wasn't paying any attention. This forced two cars in that lane to go into the center of the highway where the grass grows, and both cars began to swerve violently back and forth and back into the line of traffic, trying desperately to slow down or stop in order to miss the tractor trailer truck.

We were far enough behind not to be involved in the wreck, but I saw it all unfold before me, and the result was at least six cars crashing into each other, with headlights and taillights breaking and fenders and bumpers being smashed and twisted. I immediately pulled off the road close to the wrecked cars. I told Arielle to call 911 right away and tell them that there had been a bad accident at mile marker 200 on the southbound side of I-75 just outside of Macon, Georgia.

As I got out of my car, I could see people staggering out of their cars to lie down on the grass, obviously hurt and shocked. I told Arielle, Katie, and Robert P. Rabbit to stay in the car, and I grabbed the beach blankets we had and rushed up to provide whatever help I could and to cover the people on the side of the road who were obviously in shock. I could see that at least six cars had been damaged. The occupants were sitting in their cars with the doors open or moving around to assess the damage. Many other cars had stopped too, and many people had come to see what had happened and to offer help. With the many cars stopped, the people milling around, and the other cars trying to get around the wreckage on the freeway, the scene was very confusing.

It seemed like forever before I heard the sirens of the emergency vehicles, but I think it was probably only twenty minutes or so. Several police cars, a fire engine, and two ambulances all arrived at about the same time, and as the professionals took over the care of the injured, I backed off and watched from a little ways away.

As I watched, I heard a mother who was sitting in the open door of her car crying. "My two children are missing," she cried to the police. She explained that the crash had dazed her, and when she regained her senses and looked into the back seat of her car, the door was open and her two children were gone.

I helped as we began to frantically call for the children, but we couldn't see them anywhere since there were so many cars stopped in the road.

Just when we were about to give up looking and leave it to the emergency workers, Arielle leaned out of the car window, pointed past me, and yelled, "There they are." I turned to look where everyone was pointing, and there, twenty feet off the road in a small patch of grass, sat our dear, sweet Katie with a small child snuggled up to her in each arm, and with Robert P. Rabbit in Katie's lap.

The children, though they had some bangs and bruises, were calmly listening to Katie singing to them as they petted the soft, furry back of Robert P. Rabbit. Their mother rushed over to Katie and picked up her children, and, with tears in her eyes, thanked Katie profusely. Katie just smiled and waved goodbye to the children. They waved back at her, and then they said, "Goodbye, Robert P. Rabbit. It was nice to meet you." I couldn't tell if they had THE MARK, but I highly suspected they did.

After all the excitement, we continued on our trip as I thanked the good Lord that we weren't next to the truck when it swerved and that Katie and Robert P. Rabbit were there for the children.

CHAPTER THIRTEEN

BE GLAD FOR WHO YOU ARE

It was early evening when we arrived at the condo where we were all staying on Hilton Head Island, and we unloaded our things as quickly as we could. Polly and Arielle stayed inside to unload the food and organize who would sleep where, and the rest of us brought as many loads as necessary from the cars until everything was inside. Since we were finally at the beach, it didn't matter to anyone that we would only have a few hours of daylight left—they wanted to go to the beach right away. So I agreed, and Wendy took all the children down the pathway toward the beach as fast as they could go.

All, that is, except Katie, Robert P. Rabbit, and I, who had to go more slowly, as we had a more complicated situation facing us. We had rented a wheelchair with giant balloon-type wheels for Katie that had been delivered to the condo and was waiting for us when we checked in. Katie said it was the coolest weird wheelchair she had ever seen, as it could easily go on the sand of the beach without too much effort. It was a little harder to negotiate down the wooden boardwalk, but soon I got the hang of it.

Robert P. Rabbit rode in Katie's lap; he was not about to risk trying to hop along beside the wheelchair. He wasn't sure what strange animals and creatures might be hidden in the underbrush on either side of the walkway that might decide to have rabbit for dinner.

These wonderful wooden boardwalks run the hundred or so yards from the condos to the beach at Hilton Head Island, right through the palmettos, swamps, and natural marshlands of this tropical paradise. Everything is as natural as can be, and there are animals in abundance. So Robert P. Rabbit was wise to be very careful, as a rabbit would certainly be on the menu of some of these creatures.

"Slow down, GrandDad," Katie said. "I want to look at what we might see along the way."

The walkway was at least five feet or so above the marsh, with palmetto plants, standing water, grass, and palm trees everywhere. But every so often we saw a patch of ground above the water that had been dried by the sun. And often there would be animals on these patches of dry ground.

"Look there," Katie cried. "An alligator."

"What is an alligator?" asked Robert P. Rabbit. "It looks like a rather ugly and mean creature, if you ask me," he said.

"Well, it is kind of a great big lizard that lives in the swamps," said Katie.

"It has awfully big teeth, and it doesn't look like it eats

grass and blueberries to stay alive," said Robert P. Rabbit, "so I don't think I want to go near one of those. I hope they don't come out on the beach where we will be playing."

"Don't worry," said Katie. "They don't ever come out on the beach, especially since there is a chain link fence between this marsh and the beach. But you are right about what they eat. It's not grass. They eat birds, fish, turtles, and small animals, so you don't want to go near one of them."

"Well you don't need to worry about that," said Robert P. Rabbit. "I have better sense than to do that."

"And look over there," said Katie. "A beautiful blue heron."

"That's a funny looking creature," said Robert P. Rabbit. "I suppose it is a bird, but it sure isn't like any bird I've ever seen. It has such long legs, and such a long neck, and such a long beak," he added.

"That's so it can stand up in the shallow water and lean way out to see the fish, and then use its long beak and neck to catch the fish," said Katie.

"Sounds like a good plan to me. That is. if you're a tall skinny bird that likes fish," said Robert P. Rabbit. "But I wouldn't want to have to try to stand up in the water on my long legs all the time, and I certainly couldn't stretch my neck high enough to see a fish, let alone catch it in my mouth if I did see it. I'm glad God made me to be satisfied with carrots and an occasional rutabaga," he said. "I certainly wouldn't want to be as mean as the alligator eating my fuzzy little friends, and I'm certainly glad I'm not as funny looking as a bird that has to catch fish every time he's hungry," he added.

"When you think about it," said Katie, "that bird is probably glad she isn't you, either. She probably thinks you are a funny looking animal who eats very strange things."

"Well, I declare," said Robert P. Rabbit. "She has her nerve, calling me funny looking. Why, I once won a prize at the county fair as the best looking rabbit in the show. I even got a blue ribbon to prove it," he added very proudly.

"Oh, Robert P. Rabbit," said Katie, "I think you are the most handsomest rabbit I've ever seen, and I'm certainly glad you are not an alligator or a blue heron."

We moved slowly along the boardwalk, looking at turtles, snakes, and a variety of beautiful birds, and we even saw a small deer. We were having such a good time seeing all the wildlife and answering Robert P. Rabbit's questions that we forgot completely about going out to the beach.

Before we knew it, it was getting dark, and everyone who had run down to the beach earlier came running back up the walkway. When they got to the condo, they told Polly all the wonderful things they had seen and how they couldn't wait for tomorrow to play on the beach in the sunshine.

Robert P. Rabbit was a little disappointed that he had not yet seen the ocean, but his head was so full of new information that he was glad he had something to look forward to the next day, as he now knew about lots of new creatures that he didn't want to meet face to face. I told him there was no danger in that, so he could stop worrying.

By then, wonderful Polly and helpful Arielle had supper ready on the table for everyone.

"What did you learn along the boardwalk, Katie?" Polly asked.

"Oh, Robert P. Rabbit and I learned that we are very glad that God made us who we are, and didn't make us someone else," she said, "and Robert P. Rabbit found out that he does not want to have to catch fish or dodge alligators like a blue heron has to do."

"Well he certainly doesn't have to do that," said Polly. "And to prove it, I bought him an especially good rutabaga for dinner." She gave the rutabaga to Robert P. Rabbit along with a love pinch on his ear. In return, Robert P. Rabbit gave Polly a wink with his pink eye, of course meaning that Polly was now a special person in the world of Robert P. Rabbit, as he never gave a wink with his pink eye to anyone except very special people. I'm still getting winks with his blue eye.

CHAPTER FOURTEEN

LOST AND FOUND

The next day started as a bright and cheery morning. Katie came into my room very early, before anyone else was up, and whispered in my ear, "GrandDad, are you awake?"

Of course with her that close to me, there was no way I was going to be anything but awake, so I said, "Yes, I'm awake, honey. Is it sunny out?"

"Oh yes, GrandDad, it is beautiful out, and I can tell it is going to be a perfect day at the beach."

"Where is Robert P. Rabbit?" I said.

"He is out on the balcony looking at the ocean and asking me lots and lots of questions, but I just don't have lots and lots of answers," she responded. "I told him that as soon as you got up, you would go out and answer his questions for him."

"OK," I said, "Let me get dressed, and I'll be right out. But first I think we will need to have some breakfast."

"Oh, do we have to have breakfast? It will take so long, and I want to get out to the beach as soon as possible," she said with a frown.

"Yes, Katie, we have to have breakfast or we won't have the energy to make it through the day with all we will be doing," I responded.

So I got dressed, woke Polly, and went out into the great room. To my surprise, the room was full of all the kids, who were acting like it was Christmas morning. Mary Brooks and Parker were shooting plastic arrows at each other, Emily was drawing pictures on Polly's magazines and putting them on the walls with scotch tape, Will was trying to set up a Big Wheels track that everyone kept knocking over, and Arielle was trying to set up a line of dominos to push over from one end so they would all fall down in sequence. Everyone had their swimsuits on already, and they had gotten out all of the beach toys, but none of the essential items, such as the cooler, the water bottles, the towels, the beach chairs, or the beach umbrella.

To escape the chaos in the room, I decided to retreat to the balcony where I found Robert P. Rabbit. Since we were on the third floor of the building, we had a wonderful view of the beach and the ocean one hundred or so yards away. I could tell that he had been contemplating the scene all morning, and I prepared myself for Robert P. Rabbit's usual flurry of questions.

"Good morning," he said. "I hope you are well rested, because from the looks of the bunch you have brought with you to the beach, you are going to need all the strength you can muster just to keep up with them. Do you have a plan to restore order, or are you just going to continue to let things keep getting out of hand?"

Well, this approach was a surprise. I was expecting questions, and what I heard sounded like Polly speaking, not Robert P. Rabbit. But before I could reply, Polly came out, took me by the arm, and pulled me into the condo, saying, "GrandDad, I need you to turn on the TV to calm everyone down, set the table for breakfast, get everything ready to take to the beach, and make sure everyone has sunscreen on. I'll go make breakfast."

I just stood there not knowing what to do first and wondering how I got into such a mess so early in the morning, when all I had done so far was get dressed. Just then, Katie came over to me and said, "Don't worry, GrandDad, I'll help you, and so will the others. We don't want you to have to do all these things all by yourself. I'll turn on *Bubble Guppies* for the young ones, Emily will put sunscreen on everyone, Will will gather the beach things, and Parker will fill the cooler with ice. Working together, we will have this done in no time."

And Katie was right. By the time Polly had breakfast ready, we were all prepared for the beach, and it took no time for everyone to eat, run out the door, and race down the walkway—except, of course, for Katie, Robert P. Rabbit, and me. Because we were taking Katie's wheelchair, we volunteered to take most of the beach items. That gave us a little more time to talk while we walked, and it gave Robert P. Rabbit a chance to ask some of his questions.

"What holds the water back?" he asked. "Why doesn't it just keep coming on in and cover up all the land around us?"

"Well, it's like a puddle of water on the ground after a rain. The puddle settles into the dips in the ground, and the higher land around it holds the puddle in place," I answered. "The ocean is just a very big puddle, and the sand is higher than the ocean, so the sand keeps the ocean in its place where it belongs."

"You don't say," he said. "And what makes the waves come in?"

"When you drop a rock into the puddle, do you remember how little circles of small waves come out from where the rock hit the water to the edge of the puddle? Well, no one is dropping big rocks into the ocean, but out in the middle of the ocean there is a strong wind blowing, and the wind pushes the waves across the ocean to the shore, where they break on the sand."

"You don't say," he said. "Does anything live in the ocean?"

"Yes, just like the lakes and rivers in North Georgia, there are fish, crabs, snails, and lots of creatures of all kinds. Only some of them are very large and very dangerous, like sharks and electric eels."

"You don't say," he said.

We arrived at the beach and Katie asked if she could get out of her wheelchair to play in the sand. I said yes, if she promised to ask permission before playing away from our beach chairs. I found a good spot near where the other children were already playing, and I used a hammer to drive the tube that would hold the umbrella into the sand. I made the umbrella slant so that the wind from the ocean wouldn't lift up the umbrella and carry it away. I set out the towels so the children would have a place to lie down if they wanted to. I filled a cup with ice and cold water; I set up a lounge chair for Polly, who pulled out her latest Karen Kingsbury novel and started reading; I put Robert P. Rabbit on top of the cooler; and I settled down to watch the children playing in front of me.

After riding the waves for a little while and generally enjoying splashing and playing in the ocean waves, the group decided to build a sand castle. Not any ordinary sand castle, but the biggest and best sand castle on the entire beach. To start with, they took their beach shovels and dug a really big trench in a circle that was wider than I am tall. All but a very few waves would fail to reach the trench, but about every seventh wave reached it, and when it did, the trench would fill with water, making a wonderful moat to surround their sand castle.

They then filled their biggest bucket with wet sand and turned it upside down, and when they lifted the bucket, they had a wonderful tower of sand. They did this several times to make a solid base for their castle, and the last bucket was set up on top of the first towers, so the top of their castle was then two buckets high. In a circle around this large structure, they made smaller towers and found shells to make windows in the towers and to decorate their castle. They even dug tunnels where they said the princes and the princesses would arrive for the great ball they would have in their castle. But they decided that something was missing. They needed a king for their castle.

Mary Brooks found a horseshoe crab shell, and she offered it for the king, but no one wanted a crab for a king (although they decided that some Kings were probably quite "crabby").

Will found a conch shell, but they decided that conch shells were only used to blow warnings or to announce the arrival of an important person, so the conch shell couldn't be the king.

Emily found some starfish, but they used those to further decorate the sand castle and not to be king.

Finally Katie had a brilliant idea: Robert P. Rabbit could be their king. Everyone squealed with delight. That was just the right decision. Robert P. Rabbit would make an excellent King for their castle. So they came running up to us and put the question to Robert P. Rabbit.

"Would you be our king?" they asked.

"I'm not sure that I want to be a king," he said. "What would my duties be?"

"Well," they said, "we will put you on the tallest tower of the castle, and you will rule over all that you see. No one can come into the castle without your permission, and you will be able to order everyone to serve your every need."

This began to sound pretty good to Robert P. Rabbit— especially the part about everyone serving him, so he consented to be the king of their castle. He made himself inanimate so passersby would not know he was a real rabbit, and they took him to the tower where they carefully placed him in the place of honor. Before going, however, it occurred to him that he was going to be very close to the ocean, and I had told him about the tide that came in every day and pulled the ocean further onto the shore. He wisely deduced that the ocean could very well wash away the castle if the waves came in far enough, so he said to Katie, "If the castle starts to wash away, will you be sure I am not washed out into the ocean?"

"Of course I will," she said.

After Robert P. Rabbit was put onto the top tower, everyone who came by said that the castle was the finest sand castle on the beach and that their king was certainly the most majestic king they had seen. However, soon Robert P. Rabbit decided that this king thing wasn't all it was cracked up to be. Not only was no one serving him anything, but also it soon became evident that completed castles, with a stuffed rabbit on the top tower, don't really do anything, and cease to be very interesting to playing children.

As a result, as soon as the children saw that Mary Brooks was catching small fish in a nearby tidal pool, they lost interest in the castle and in its royal king. Off they all went to

catch fish in their nets to put into their buckets, which they
had filled with water. Robert P. Rabbit realized not only that
he was now all alone, but also that the dreaded tide was coming in and washing over the moat, eating away at the towers.
In fact, the towers were all disappearing into the ocean at a
rapid pace, and it would not be long before the very tower he
was sitting on would disintegrate and be gone.

From where I sat, I could see all of this developing, and as
I caught Robert P. Rabbit's eye, I knew he wanted me to distract the passersby so he could turn himself back into a real
rabbit and get out of there without being chased by passing
children. Since I didn't relish the idea of getting into the water if I could help it, I immediately shouted, "Look!" while
pointing into the sky at a passing helicopter. Everyone knows
that if you yell, "Look," and then point into the sky, everyone around you will look exactly where you are pointing,
and that is what they all did. So for that brief instant, while

everyone was looking up, Robert P. Rabbit took three big jumps from his high tower (which was getting lower all the time) and landed right in my lap. I quickly covered him with a towel, and tried to look as normal as I could, as if nothing out of the ordinary had happened, and everyone around me just kept walking. In the meantime, not only the castle tower, but also the entire kingdom the children had built, collapsed into the foamy, swirling surf and disappeared.

As all of this excitement was very taxing on Robert P. Rabbit, he decided to take a little nap, and he was soon fast asleep in my lap under the towel. (I kept him covered so people who passed by would not think that I always kept a rabbit in my lap, like some small child would do.) I found myself dozing off, too.

In the meantime, it finally occurred to Katie that she needed to check on Robert P. Rabbit to be sure he was all right. When she looked at where the castle had been, she could see that the waves had totally overtaken it, and it, along with Robert P. Rabbit, was gone. What a terrible feeling it was for Katie.

"Oh Emily," she cried. "The castle is gone, and so is Robert P. Rabbit! He must have washed into the ocean, and maybe a shark has eaten him. What will we do?"

So all of the children began to look out into the ocean to see if they could spot Robert P. Rabbit's little ears floating above the waves. They ran up and down the beach looking, but to no avail. They asked everyone in the area if they had seen a little white rabbit, but no one had seen him. Finally

Katie just sat down on the beach and began to cry. Emily tried to comfort her, but it was no use; Katie couldn't stand the idea that Robert P. Rabbit had become some fish's lunch.

At that time Polly came out from the condo, bringing lunch with her. She saw the two girls sitting on the beach crying and then looked down at me, seeing that I was not totally awake.

"GrandDad," she said rather loudly, startling me awake from a half sleep, "I thought you were watching the children."

"I am," I said meekly.

"You looked like you were asleep to me," she said.

"It was just a catnap," I said sheepishly, as if catnaps were OK, not being the real thing.

"Then why are the girls crying?" she asked.

Well that woke me up for sure, as I had no idea why, or even if, someone was crying.

"I was just about to go find out," I said, knowing for sure that she knew better.

However, to show my sincerity, I jumped out of the beach chair, forgetting about Robert P. Rabbit, and he came flying out of my lap and onto the sand with a jolt.

"Now look what you've done," she said as she picked up Robert P. Rabbit and lovingly cradled him in her arms, brushing the sand off his little body. Actually, it was very satisfying to see Polly's concern for Robert P. Rabbit, and I was distracted by it for a minute or two. But when I regained my senses, I continued on my quest to find out why the girls were crying, so I went to them sitting in the sand.

"What's the matter, girls?" I said.

"We've lost Robert P. Rabbit, and we are afraid he washed out to sea and a shark has eaten him!" cried Katie.

I knew right away what had happened.

"Girls, when you think you have lost something you really love, how does it make you feel?" I asked.

"Very sad," they said, "and it makes us even sadder that there were so many things we wanted to say to him, and do with him, and do for him, and now it's too late."

"And if you found him again, what would you do?" I asked.

"We'd do all those things, and we'd let him know just how special he is to us. But he's gone, GrandDad, so we won't have the chance."

"Yes, you will," I said, "because he's not gone. He saved himself, and he is with Polly over there right now."

With that they looked up, saw Robert P. Rabbit in Polly's arms, and ran as fast as they could—even Katie without her wheelchair—to Polly, where they hugged Robert P. Rabbit so much, and so hard, that he thought he wasn't going to be able to breathe.

Later that night, when I was saying prayers with Katie, she said, "GrandDad, isn't it ever so special when something that you thought was lost is found again? I don't think there is much of anything that can make me any happier." And I had to agree with her.

CHAPTER FIFTEEN

THE GREAT HILTON HEAD ISLAND BIKE RIDE

It was a beautiful, sunny day on Hilton Head Island, a perfect day for a bike ride. At Hilton Head there are miles and miles of bike trails, so I rented bikes for Arielle, Will, and me, and I rented a carriage for Katie that attached to my bike so I could pull Katie along. Unfortunately Emily and Mary Brooks had to go back to Mississippi, but we were prepared to have as much fun as we could in spite of their absence. At breakfast that morning we four sat at the table and planned where we wanted to ride.

"I want to go by the ponds to see the alligators," said Katie. "When we drove onto the Island when we first got here, there were alligators just sitting on the banks at almost all the little ponds that I could see along the road. And the bike paths go by a lot of these little ponds."

"Why do you want to see those ugly, mean looking creatures?" said Robert P. Rabbit to Katie. "And why are they just sitting on the bank? Why aren't they in the water where it's cool?"

"Well," said Katie, "alligators are cold blooded creatures, so their blood doesn't keep them warm like our blood does for us, so they come out of the water when the sun shines so they can soak up the heat from the sun. That's why you don't see alligators much further north than we are right now, because it is too cold for them."

"Don't worry," I said. "We will see alligators whether we want to or not. The bike paths all go by ponds, and every pond down here is going to have an alligator or two in it."

So having solved the issue of the alligators, we went back to planning just where we would go on our bike ride. We elected Arielle as our guide, as she was the tallest and could see what was coming ahead better than Will, and she wouldn't be pulling a carriage. Polly packed a lunch for each of us in case we stayed out a long time, and she gave us each a water bottle to carry in the basket that was on the handle bar of each bike. Robert P. Rabbit decided that Katie would have to carry Will's lunch, as he wanted to ride in Will's basket rather than in the chair with Katie.

"If I ride with Katie, I won't be able to see as much because I will be so low down," he said. "Now, you know how to ride one of these bikes, Will, don't you?" he asked. "I'm not interested in being involved in a bike crash, or being run over by a car, or ending up in a thorn bush."

"Oh I know how to ride really well," said Will. "My dad taught me how to ride last Thursday, so by now I am really experienced."

"What?" exclaimed Robert P. Rabbit. "Last Thursday! That means you haven't even been riding for a full week, and really even less than that since we have been on the road or here at the beach for most of that time. I've changed my mind, I don't think I want to ride in your basket."

"Will," said Katie, "you know that isn't true. You have been riding your bike for at least three or four years. Don't listen to him, Robert P. Rabbit; he is the best rider in our family. He even went down the mountain bike trail in Tallulah Falls. Now, Will, don't say things that aren't true. People won't believe you when you really need them to if you don't tell the truth all the time. Don't you remember the story of the boy who cried wolf? He cried wolf so many times when there wasn't really a wolf there that the people stopped coming to help him when he cried out. Then when there really was a wolf after him, and he cried for help, no one came to help him, and the wolf got him."

"Yeah," said Robert P. Rabbit, "when you yell for help because the alligator is after you, I won't believe you and I won't come to help."

"How could you help me if an alligator is after me?" said Will. "You would be no match for an alligator."

"Oh, you would be surprised," said Robert P. Rabbit. And in fact, soon Robert P. Rabbit would have the chance to prove it to Will, and to everyone else.

With our planning finished, we all went out to the bikes so we could start our great Hilton Head Island bike adventure.

First, we rode around in circles in the parking lot for a few turns so we could all get used to our bikes, and then we headed out to the bike trails. The trails all crossed roads from time to time, so we had to be very careful to watch out for cars coming on the side roads trying to get out onto the main road. Arielle was very careful to stop our little line of bikes if a car was coming and was very good at stopping in the road until all of us got across, and then she would catch up to take the lead again until we came to another road. Just as I told them, lots of alligators were sunning themselves at almost every pond we passed. And there was a beautiful golf course along the way where golfers were driving golf carts and putting their little golf balls on beautiful greens. Each green had a flag in the middle sticking out of a small hole about the size of a baseball, and the golfers were each trying to putt their little white golf balls into these little holes before another golfer on the green could do it. Fortunately, no one asked me why these grown men were hitting their little white golf balls all over the place and trying to get them into the little holes, as I don't think I could have explained that very well.

Our destination for the trip was the boat harbor with the beautiful red and white lighthouse that was the symbol of Hilton Head Island. I had shown them the pictures of the lighthouse, and they were all very anxious to see it firsthand. Will was the first to spot it, so he won the prize I offered to the first person to see it.

"What do I win, GrandDad?" he asked.

I pulled out the prize from my basket and handed it to him.

"Wow," he yelled. "A genuine Spider-Man combination pocket knife, compass, and magnifying glass with a hidden flashlight in the handle!"

"What's so great about that?" asked Robert P. Rabbit.

"It's just the coolest knife ever made," said Will. "You just wait and see; you'll be glad I have it one of these days."

"What is the lighthouse for?" asked Katie

"Well," I said, "when it is night, or there is a dense fog over the water, and boats are trying to get into the harbor, the lighthouse will shine its light out over the water so the boats will know just where the harbor is and won't run into the rocks along the shore. It has saved many sailors all along any coast for many years. In the past, before electricity, the lighthouses would have giant candles at the top, with big mirrors to reflect the light. They still have the mirrors, but the light now is a big light bulb, rather than a candle."

We rode on into the harbor and got off our bikes to walk around and see the cool boats that were docked there. Some of them looked like floating hotels, they were so big. Some had sailboats with masts as high as a two-story building, and some were called yachts, because they could sleep five or ten people below their main decks and had chairs and tables out in the open areas where the passengers could gather to eat and talk as the boat cruised along.

Next to the harbor there were picnic tables, so we broke out the lunches Polly had made and ate our lunch before starting back to the condo. Arielle went on ahead so she could help Polly get ready for dinner, while the rest of us took our time.

On the ride back, as we got close to our parking lot, Katie yelled, "Stop, everyone!"

She yelled so loudly that I immediately put on my brakes and turned around to look, expecting to see the worst, but there was Katie pointing toward the pond right next to the bike path.

"Look," she said, "over there by that big Oleander bush. Do you see that little baby duck?"

"I see it," said Will.

"Well, watch what it is doing," said Katie. "It keeps running out into the open and grabbing something, and then running back under the bush. Then it runs out again and does the same thing all over again. And look at that alligator watching the duck. He looks like he is going to leap out and grab the little fellow as soon as he gets close enough."

We continued to watch as at least five more baby ducks did the same thing, running out from under the bush, grabbing something, and running back under the bush for safety.

"GrandDad, I think the little ducks need our help," said Katie. "I know what we'll do. Robert P. Rabbit, will you hop over there under the bush and see if you can tell what's happening? But be very careful of that alligator."

"I can do that," he said. And he jumped out of the basket and carefully hopped over to the bush. Because the little ducks must be used to being around rabbits, they didn't seem to mind it at all when he went under the bush. He stayed there for a few minutes, and then came hopping back, being very careful to stay clear of the alligator.

"What did you see?" asked Katie.

"We must go back to the condo and discuss this," said Robert P. Rabbit. "I think those little ducks need our help very badly, and we have to provide it correctly so that we don't do more harm than good."

So back to the condo we all went so that Katie, Will, and Robert P. Rabbit could plan their next move.

And a wonderful, helpful, and humanitarian move it was, if I do say so myself, but not without a certain element of danger involved.

CHAPTER SIXTEEN

KATIE, WILL AND ROBERT P. RABBIT BECOME THE GLOBAL DETECTIVES

While the rest of us began to get ready for some afternoon time at the beach, Katie, Will, and Robert P. Rabbit put their heads together to decide what they could do to help the little ducks they had just seen under the bush near our condo. First, Robert P. Rabbit had to outline for the others just what he had seen under the bush.

"OK," he said, "here's the situation. All of the little ducks we saw are members of the same family. There are eight of them, and they are only a few months old. They told me that when they were first born, they were just like all the other duck families near their pond. Their mother would take them out each day and teach them how to swim, how to stay away from the alligators, and how to avoid the humans—especially small boys who always wanted to pick them up and carry them away into all sorts of danger. Then one day while they were all under the bush, snuggled up to each other taking their afternoon nap, they heard a screech of tires, and when they looked out to see what had happened, they saw their mother limping back to the bush as fast as she could. She had been hit by a car, and one of her feet had been run over by the car's tire. When she got to the bush it was all she could do to just lie down and rest her foot. The next morning, she found that she could not walk at all on that foot."

"Oh dear," said Katie, "what a terrible thing to happen. How can she eat if she can't walk? And how can she take care of the little ones? And how can she teach them the things they need to know to survive?"

"That's the problem," said Robert P. Rabbit. "The mother didn't have time to teach them how to find food, so they have been trying to get what they can, not only for themselves, but also for their mother. When she spots a bug or a worm, she points it out to the little ducks, and they run out and grab it and bring it back for all of them to share."

"Boy, that's not going to be enough to keep them alive for very long," said Will.

"So we need to help them," said Katie. "I think we need to become detectives and find out everything we can to help solve their problem."

"How do we become detectives?" asked Will.

"I'm not sure," said Katie, "but we can go ask GrandDad. I've heard him talk about how he has used detectives before in his law practice, so he should be able to tell us how. Let's go ask him."

With that they all traipsed out to my chair on the porch where I was reading my paper and having an ice cold Coke.

"GrandDad," said Katie, "we want to become real detectives, and we need you to show us how."

"Why do you want to be detectives?" I asked.

"Well, we have a problem to solve, and we don't know where to start. We thought if we were detectives, we would know exactly how to go about solving our problem," she said. "And besides, we got a good start out in Avon where we figured out where to find Jeremy when no one else could," she added.

Well, I certainly couldn't argue with that, so I decided to do what I could to help them become real detectives.

"You are on the right track," I said "A good detective will always start by recognizing that there is a problem. He will then put down on paper all of the facts he knows concerning the problem, and then add to that what he doesn't know about the problem, and then add to that what he thinks he needs to learn about the problem and the solution, and only then can he start to solve the problem. But first, to make you real detectives we need to get you a license to be a detective. You can't just go off and start solving problems without first having a detective's license."

"How do we get a detective's license?" asked Katie.

"Well, first you need a name for your detective agency. That is what will you call your group. And then, after you have a name, you need to have some business cards you can give people when you tell them you are detectives. The cards should have your names on them, the name of your detective agency, and your phone number so that if someone needs you, they can get in touch with you. So you come up with your name, and I will go to Kinkos and get some business cards printed up for you, and then I will give you a certificate showing that you are a real detective agency."

With that they retreated into the small bedroom, which they turned into their office by stretching a blanket between the two twin beds and getting under the blanket so that they would have privacy while they created their detective agency.

"What shall we call ourselves?" asked Will.

"How about The Best Detective Agency?" suggested Katie.

"No," said Robert P. Rabbit. "That sounds like maybe the agency is owned by someone named Best. We need the name to say something about who we are, or where we live, or where we will do our detective work."

"I know," said Will. "We can be The Tallulah Falls Detectives."

"That would make people think we only solve problems in Tallulah Falls," said Robert P. Rabbit. "I think we should be at least the Georgia Detective Agency, or the USA Detective agency, since we are going to solve our first problem here in South Carolina."

"No," said Katie. "I've got it. We should let people know we are so good at being detectives we can solve problems anywhere in the world. We will be called the Global Detectives."

And that was it. They all agreed that it was a magnificent name, and they came to me right away asking me to hurry and get their business cards and certificate, as they were already working on their first case.

Back in their new office, they started going over what a good detective does.

"OK," said Katie. "Here are the things we know. The mother duck has been injured. She can't feed her ducklings.

She can't continue their swimming lessons. She can't feed herself. She needs to have her foot looked at for possible infection. The little ducks need to be protected from the alligator. She is living under the big Oleander bush. The other ducks aren't helping at all. Now, what don't we know."

"Well," said Robert P. Rabbit, "we don't know what ducks eat. We don't know if the little ducks need to be taught to swim. We don't know how long it will take for the mother's foot to heal. We don't know if their place under the bush is safe from alligators. And we don't know if they can get the food they need once we find out what it is they do need. And we don't know if the little ducks will let us help once we decide what we should do."

"So, how do we start?" asked Will.

"I think I know," said Katie. "Will, go get our computer. We need to look up some information on the Internet."

So Will went to get his computer, and Katie started her research. First she went to Google and entered the question, "What do ducks eat?" When she looked at the links she saw a site that was titled, "What to Feed Ducks."

"Look," she said. "It says here not to feed ducks bread, chips, popcorn, or crackers. It says that those things have very little food value and can actually harm a duckling's growth. Wow, that's what we always feed the ducks in the park, but it is telling us not to feed little ducks these things."

"So what can we feed them?" asked Will.

"It says the best things for ducks are cracked corn, wheat, grains, oats, rice, or birdseed," said Katie. "We can't get all of those things, but we certainly can get birdseed. Quick, go catch GrandDad before he leaves to get our business cards, and tell him we need a bag of birdseed."

"OK, Katie," said Robert P. Rabbit. "That's all well and good, but we will only be here for a week, so what do they do for food after we are gone?"

"Well, let's read more to see if we can find out what little ducks eat when people aren't around." So Katie went back to the computer and found out what ducks eat in the natural order of things.

"It says here that ducks eat lots of things they can find on their own, such as small fish and fish eggs, snails, worms, grass and weeds, frogs, insects, small berries, and all kinds of nuts and seeds. So it seems to me that all we have to do is help the little ducks find these things, and after a while they should be able to do it on their own," said Katie.

"It looks like we just did the third thing your GrandDad said a good detective does, and that is come up with a solution to the problem," said Robert P. Rabbit. "I think this detective thing is a lot of fun. Now let's get to work on the other parts of our problem."

They spent the rest of the afternoon working out solutions to all the problems faced by the mother duck and her eight little ducklings. Since it was dark when they completed their thinking and planning, they decided to wait until the next morning to go back to the ducks with all their solutions. Besides, they felt like they shouldn't do anything detectively until they had their certificate and business cards, and it was after dinner before I finally went to Kinkos.

When I came back, I called them into the living room and presented them with two things. First were their business cards. On each card were each of their names: "Katie, Will, and Robert P. Rabbit, Detectives of the Global Detective Agency," along with Katie's home phone number. Then I handed them a certificate that said:

By The Power Invested In Me
By The Sovereign State Of Georgia
I Hereby Certify That The Following Persons
Are Declared To Be
OFFICIAL DETECTIVES
In The Detective Agency Known As
THE GLOBAL DETECTIVE AGENCY
Katie Seaman, Will Seaman,
and Robert P. Rabbit
Signed, Sealed, and Delivered by
Attorney at Law—GrandDad

They couldn't wait to show their certificate to anyone who would look at it—even to all the neighbors they could find in the condo area and around the condo pool.

The next morning they were up at daybreak, and as soon as they could get Arielle to go with them, they went back to the pond where they had seen the little ducks.

First they made sure that the ducks were still there, and to their great relief, they were. Next Robert P. Rabbit went over to the bush to assure the mother duck that Katie and Will were there to help. Robert P. Rabbit could talk to the ducks, but Katie and Will couldn't, as Robert P. Rabbit said that ducks were just not as smart as Special Rabbits like him, so no duck had ever been able to talk to a human. Because no one was worried about Katie getting dizzy and falling (because if she did, she would be crawling on the ground anyway, and it wouldn't hurt her), Katie didn't need her wheelchair as she went about helping the ducks.

They first fed all the ducks the birdseed that I had gotten the night before. Then they took the ducks to the pond to put them in the water for an early morning swim. They had read that ducks didn't need to be taught to swim, they did that naturally. But they did need to be taught to swim in the early morning when the alligators were less active because they were still cold from the night chill. Will showed the little ducks how to catch little fish along the side of the pond. He used his net to catch the fish, held the fish just under the water where the little duck could put its head under and take the fish from Will's hand. Soon the little ducks were doing it on their own, much to the delight of mother duck. Every once in a while a little duck would bring a fish to their mother to be sure she had some food to help her get better.

While all of this was going on, Katie was putting some ointment on the mother duck's webbed foot to kill any infection that might be developing. She then moved the mother duck to some higher ground, further away from where the alligators hunted. She had discovered that the alligators always stayed close to the water in case they had to escape. She also learned that alligators are pretty lazy, and since they can get all the fish they want in the pond, they won't bother to climb a little hill to try to catch a duck. They could rarely catch a duck in the first place, so when the duck was as far away from the pond as Katie put this mother duck, the alligators wouldn't even bother to try to catch her or her ducklings.

After the Ducks had their swim, Will began to dig for worms. Katie thought that was icky, so she left that part to Will. After he fed a few to the ducks, they were soon scratching around all by themselves, not only finding worms, but catching all kinds of insects.

All in all, it was a very successful morning. When they got back to the condo, they couldn't stop talking about how successfully their very first detective case had gone. And a few days later, they were very pleased to go out in the morning for their daily check on the ducks to see mama duck and all eight ducklings in a row, swimming as much as they pleased in the pond. They knew then that they had been successful and were indeed the world's best Global Detectives, having solved a very difficult problem that saved the lives of nine of our wonderful feathered friends.

CHAPTER SEVENTEEN

THE TRIP TO UNCLE ERIC AND AUNT CALLIE'S

Later in the week, I received a call from my son Eric, who lives in Colorado with his wife Callie.

"Dad," he said, "Callie and I have been thinking that if Katie is up to it, we would like for her to come to Denver and visit us for awhile."

"Well, that sounds all right to me, but I will have to check with Wendy and with her doctors first," I said. "I'll call you back tonight after we have had a chance to discuss it."

I went into the kitchen where Wendy and Polly were preparing dinner. Katie, the other children, and Robert P. Rabbit were out on the porch watching a group of dolphins playing just off the beach. We were so far away that they had to use binoculars to see them, and because his eyes are much closer together than Katie's, it was hard for Robert P. Rabbit to see through the eyepieces. It was quite amusing seeing Katie trying to hold the binoculars up to his face so that he could see through them, but it was all to no avail, as he got bored with the process and declared that looking at a bunch of fish swim around in circles was a waste of time anyway.

"Wendy," I said, "Eric and Callie want Katie to come to Denver to visit them. What do you think?"

"Well, she is finished with the latest series of treatments for her cancer, and she seems to be doing fine. That sounds like fun," said Wendy. It was decided that Wendy, Katie, Will, and Robert P. Rabbit would all fly to Denver the very next week. Of course all of the others wanted to go too, but to take everyone would be entirely too expensive, and besides, Eric and Callie didn't have room at their house for that many people to sleep. They were very disappointed, but after I agreed to bring everyone to the beach again next summer, they calmed down and went back to their dolphin watching.

The rest of the time at the beach was so much fun for everyone. We swam in the ocean and in the pool; we made sand castles and took long walks on the beach; we took bike rides back to the harbor; and most importantly, we checked on the ducks every day to be sure they were all OK.

The ride back to Atlanta was a time of total peace and quiet for me, as everyone was so tired, and so baked by the sun, that they all slept the entire way back, leaving me time to plan what I wanted to do for the rest of the year. I even got the opportunity to listen to all of my favorite country music without the usual complaints from the Justin Beiber fans, who don't really understand the historical and educational benefits of the music of the mountains and the cowboy West.

Planning the trip to Denver took up the better part of a week, as Katie had to keep calling uncle Eric and aunt Callie over and over again to ask about each activity they had planned.

"We are going to hike and bike in the Rocky Mountains, walk along the most beautiful rivers you have ever seen, catch native mountain trout which we will cook over an open fire, and even camp out under beautiful stars," they told her.

"Oh my," she said, "I can hardly wait."

Finally the day came for the flight to Colorado. I took them to the airport early on Saturday morning and helped Wendy with the luggage. Because Robert P. Rabbit was an old hat at flying, he hardly had any questions at all this time, and he settled into Katie's backpack like any other good stuffed animal and promptly fell asleep. Wendy told us that he slept all the way to Denver and didn't come out of his "stuffed rabbit" mode until they were at Eric and Callie's, alone in the bedroom.

"Are you going to tell them about me?" asked Robert P. Rabbit.

"Yes," said Katie, "I think it is best if I tell them the truth. Then there won't be so many questions when I talk to you, or when you change to look like a stuffed animal. Right now they think you are my toy rabbit, but when you start hopping around the house, they are going to know something is up."

Ever since Robert P. Rabbit came to live at our house, he has found it necessary to change from time to time into a "stuffed rabbit" look, and many times it has been noticed by Polly. And even though she can't hear Robert P. Rabbit, she somehow seems to know that he really is talking to me, Katie, Emily, and Will. And she knows that sometimes he doesn't look real, but she just lets that pass, because she knows that is what's best for Robert P. Rabbit, and for Katie. She figured that out the first time I brought Robert P. Rabbit to the hospital, and after that she would bring him there herself, never once commenting on his amazing ability.

"How should we do it?" asked Katie.

"I have a plan," said Robert P. Rabbit. "Just take me into the den, and ask them to bring in their big ugly dog Bridger"

"That's terrible, Robert P. Rabbit," she said. "Bridger isn't ugly; he is beautiful. In fact, he is the most beautifulist dog I've ever seen. He is a purebred Bernese Mountain dog, and he came to them all the way from Germany when he was a puppy. You had better not call him ugly to his face, or he might get mad and do something bad to you."

"Don't worry about me," he said. "Don't you remember what I did to Pepper? This creature will be a piece of cake. Just don't get worried when he sees me come alive. I'm going to let him bark and jump around a little before I calm him down so they will see that I can mean business when I want to. And since neither Eric nor Callie will be able to talk to me, you will have to explain to them the two things I intend to do: first, that I will come alive, and second, that I will

calm down that big ug—whoops, I mean that big beauuuuti-
ful dog of theirs," he added.

So Katie picked up Robert P. Rabbit, and after he made
himself look for all the world like a stuffed rabbit, she went
out into the den to see Uncle Eric and Aunt Callie.

"Hi, Katie," said Callie as she came into the room. "Are
you all settled in your room?"

"Yes, ma'am," said Katie.

"Can we get you anything?" said Uncle Eric.

"No—on second thought, yes," said Katie. "You can go
get Bridger and bring him into the room. There is something
very serious I need to tell you, and I need Bridger here to do
it properly."

"This sounds very serious," said Callie.

"It is," said Katie. "Maybe the most serious thing you have
heard in a long time."

"Well, why do you need Bridger?" asked Eric.

"If you will go get him and bring him here, you will understand completely. At least, I hope you will," said Katie.

Eric and Callie were all ears now. They couldn't wait to
hear what Katie had to say, so they wasted no time in going
to get Bridger.

Wendy was in the room, but she had heard this all before, so she knew pretty much what Katie was going to say. While she didn't have THE MARK, she had seen enough to know the truth. In fact, she was very proud that Katie and her son Will both had THE MARK, which made them very special in her eyes. So she just sat in the back of the room, excited about what she knew was going to happen.

They brought Bridger into the room and settled him at Katie's feet. Bridger really loved Katie, and from the minute she walked into the house, he couldn't stay away from her, constantly rubbing up against her and licking her hands, legs, and anything else he could get his tongue on. She started her story.

First she explained how I had first spotted Robert P. Rabbit under the bush, and how he could talk to me because I had THE MARK, and how I could talk to him, but that Polly didn't have THE MARK, so she couldn't hear him or talk to him. Then she described how he had calmed down Pepper, and had discovered that she, Katie, has THE MARK, so she can communicate with him. She next told them about some of the adventures she and Robert P. Rabbit had had.

Since she once glanced up and saw Eric roll his eyes at Wendy, Katie knew that they didn't really believe her but rather thought that she was just imagining these things, so she knew it was time to take it to the second level.

She told them to come over and hold Robert P. Rabbit. They both did as she asked by coming over to hold him for a minute or two. Then she asked them to sit down. She told them she didn't want them to fall over with surprise when Robert P. Rabbit did his first trick.

Robert P. Rabbit knew it was now his time to take over. So as they both looked on with amazement, Robert P. Rabbit stretched out his front legs, gave a big yawn, pushed up on his back legs, and wiggled those big rabbit ears of his. So they wouldn't think that he was some kind of a mechanical rabbit, he then took a giant leap and landed right in Eric's lap. Eric jumped out of his chair, causing Robert P. Rabbit to fall to the floor.

At that moment Bridger came to life. He started barking and immediately leaped at where Robert P. Rabbit had landed, and the chase was on. Robert P. Rabbit ran from room to room, followed closely by Bridger, followed closely by Eric, followed closely by Callie. Being a really smart rabbit, Robert P. Rabbit led Bridger on a such merry chase that went in and out of all the rooms, that poor Bridger didn't know if he was coming or going. In fact, once Robert P. Rabbit ended up behind Bridger, and Bridger, being totally confused, actually stopped and stepped aside so that Robert P. Rabbit could get by him.

Now, you have to understand that Bridger is a really big dog. He weighs at least 110 pounds. So when he is running around in the house, everything is in danger: tables, chairs, dishes, lamps, and anything not on a high shelf. So Robert P. Rabbit decided it was time to stop. He had made his point, so he jumped back up into Katie's lap. Bridger slid to a stop in front of Katie, crouched and ready to spring into action.

Katie asked Eric and Callie to sit down so she could con-tinue. Eric said he thought he should hold onto Bridger, but Katie asked him not to. They were so dumbfounded that they just sat down on the couch. They couldn't take their eyes off this rabbit that had turned out to be very much alive.

"Now," said Katie, "another of Robert P. Rabbit's skills is that he can calm down any domestic animal, no matter how big the animal is, and that will include Bridger."

Actually, Katie wasn't sure Robert P. Rabbit could calm down Bridger, since he was so big. But she didn't like to doubt him, so she sat back to watch Robert P. Rabbit along with Eric and Callie.

Robert P. Rabbit stared very intently at Bridger. He then raised his ears to their highest, which wasn't something he did very often. They usually were laid down over his shoul-ders out of the way. As he raised them over his head, he wig-gled them in just a certain way, and at the same time he wig-gled his nose. Then he hopped off Katie's lap to sit on the floor right under Bridger's nose.

Bridger just sat there looking very much confused. Instead of barking, he was silent, and he tipped his head to the side as he looked down at Robert P. Rabbit. At that moment Rob-ert P. Rabbit took a small hop and landed on Bridger's paw. Bridger lay down on the floor with his nose gently pushed up into Robert P. Rabbit's fur. Robert P. Rabbit placed his front paw on Bridger's nose, and the two of them seemed to be communicating in some way that no one else in the room could understand.

After what seemed like a long time, but which was really about thirty seconds, Robert P. Rabbit circled Bridger, climbed up on his back, and then jumped back into Katie's lap. Bridger never moved, but let Robert P. Rabbit go anywhere he wanted to go. Callie and Eric just sat there and stared, not knowing just what to say.

"I know how you feel," said Wendy. "I felt the same way when Katie and Robert P. Rabbit first told me all you have heard. But as time has gone on, I have watched Katie, Emily, Will, GrandDad, and Robert P. Rabbit do all their incredible things, and I have stopped being amazed. The best advice I can give you is to just watch, and be ready for the unexpected, and you won't be disappointed. Katie now lives in a world we don't quite understand, but she and Robert P. Rabbit will make your days more fun than you can imagine."

With that, Katie and Robert P. Rabbit got up from their chair and went back to the bedroom. "Goodnight, Aunt

Callie and Uncle Eric, and goodnight, Mommy," said Katie. "See you in the morning."

"Goodnight, Katie, and goodnight, Robert P. Rabbit," said Callie.

Right after Katie left the room, Wendy, Callie, and Eric started a long conversation about what they had just seen.

"That's just the most amazing thing I have ever seen," said Callie. "I don't know whether I am dreaming, or if I somehow missed something that could explain it all to me in some sensible manner."

"Don't even try to figure it out," said Wendy. "Just accept the fact that Robert P. Rabbit is like no other animal you have ever seen and enjoy it. I am just glad that he came along and that he and Katie get along so well together."

"How long do you think he will stay?" asked Eric. "I kind of get the impression that he might be on loan to Katie, and that once she gets better, he might go away. You know, I can remember stories that GrandDad used to tell us about special animals that were around just when we needed them, and after they had completed their task with us, they went to help another child."

"I remember that, too," said Wendy. "In fact, I remember GrandDad telling me stories when I was a little girl about a special raccoon that came around our house at night and protected us from all kinds of creatures that might want to harm us. He even guarded our tent when we spent the night in the backyard. I always felt so safe because he was there. And one time, as I was getting older, I told GrandDad that I didn't think the raccoon was really ever there, and lo and behold, he woke me up a 2:00 a.m. one night and took me outside, and there he was, right on the deck eating some food Grand-Dad had put out for him earlier in the evening. When I woke up the next morning, I couldn't decide if I was dreaming the whole thing, but when I went outside, sure enough just off the deck, in the muddy ground, were the footprints of a big raccoon. From that time on I never doubted when Grand-Dad would tell me about special animals and birds he knew. Now I'm more convinced then ever that he was always telling the truth."

"I'll bet you anything that he had something to do with the sudden appearance of Robert P. Rabbit," said Eric.

"Well, don't do anything to break the spell of what Katie and this wonderful rabbit have going," said Callie. "Let's just accept the fact that we are witnesses to a miracle and enjoy every minute of our time with Robert P. Rabbit."

And that is just what all three of them decided to do.

CHAPTER EIGHTEEN

SHRINE PASS ADVENTURE

The next morning when she woke up, Katie was a little worried about what Uncle Eric and Aunt Callie were going to say about what they had seen the night before.

"Don't worry about it," said Robert P. Rabbit. "I could tell that your mom was going to handle every doubt they might have, and by this morning they will be fine, I'm sure."

Katie wasn't so sure, but she decided to dress and go out into the kitchen as if nothing out of the ordinary had happened. Robert P. Rabbit and Bridger, who had spent the night snuggled up to each other as if they were lifelong friends, went out first. By the time Katie was dressed, she could smell the bacon cooking and hear the eggs frying. Uncle Eric made the best bacon in the world. He baked it in the stove, rather than cooking it in the frying pan, and it always came out crisp and perfectly done that way.

"Wow, Uncle Eric, that sure does smell good," she said, hoping that he wouldn't bring up what he had seen the night before.

"Sit down, Katie," said Aunt Callie, "and I'll get you some eggs and some orange juice to go with the bacon. Wendy, why don't you see if Bridger and Robert P. Rabbit want to come in now and get their breakfast?"

So Wendy went to the back door and called Bridger and Robert P. Rabbit in just like they were two children playing in the yard, which they were actually doing. And sure enough, as soon as they heard her call, in they came. Bridger went right away to his bowl of dog food, and Robert P. Rabbit just sat there looking at Wendy as if to say, "Where is my food?"

"Oh, Robert P. Rabbit," said Aunt Callie, "your food is out in the hall next to Bridger's water bowl. I went to the store last night and got you some fresh lettuce and a few carrots."

As soon as she said that, Robert P. Rabbit hopped out of the kitchen and straight into the hall to where his food was waiting. With that Katie knew that Aunt Callie and Uncle Eric had accepted Robert P. Rabbit as a full fledged member of the household, and there would be no more doubt that this was one amazing rabbit.

After breakfast everyone sat at the dining room table while Uncle Eric got out the map of Colorado to show where they would go to have their hike that day.

"We are going up to the Sawatch Range of mountains today," he said, "to a place called Vail Pass. It is over 10,000 feet above sea level."

"What does that mean?" asked Katie.

"When your mom wants to see how tall you are, what does she do?" asked Uncle Eric.

"She gets out the tape measure, puts one end on the floor, pulls the other end up to the top of my head, and then reads what the number is right there at the top. I'm up to four feet two inches now," said Katie.

"Well, that is the same thing we do when we want to know how high a mountain is. To say it is 10,000 feet above sea level, it means that if you could put one end of a tape measure right on the ocean, and then pull the other end up as high as this pass is, the tape measure would measure a little over 10,000 feet."

"Is there really a tape measure that high?" asked Katie.

"No, not really," said Uncle Eric, "but there are fancy scientific instruments that can tell us how high the mountains are. We will drive up to the pass, and then we will leave the paved road and drive about five miles up a dirt road to another pass, called Shrine Pass, that is over 11,000 feet above sea level."

"What's a pass?" asked Katie.

"It's a name that they give to a break in a mountain that lets you go from one side of the mountain to the other without having to go all the way over the mountain. If we had to go to the very top of these mountains to get to the other side, we would have to go over 14,000 feet above sea level."

"Wow, thank goodness for the pass," said Katie. " I wouldn't want to have to climb that far up just to get to the other side of a mountain."

"Neither would I," said Aunt Callie.

"OK," said uncle Eric, "I want to be sure we have everything we need for the hike. First, Katie, we will take your wheelchair, since part of the hike is wheelchair accessible, and I want everyone to have a bottle of water. It is very dry here in the Rockies, so we need to drink lots of water. And Callie will carry energy bars in her backpack and a packed lunch for everyone. Wendy, you will carry jackets for you, Will and Katie, as it might be a little cold up on the mountain. I will carry a first aid kit in case someone gets hurt, and a blanket in case someone slips and falls and needs to be covered up while help comes. Bridger will have a pack that will carry our map and our GPS locator."

"What will I carry, Uncle Eric? I have my backpack with me," asked Katie.

"Oh, you will carry Robert P. Rabbit in your backpack. I don't think he wants to run around up there where there are coyotes and mountain lions that would love to have a rabbit for dinner," he said. "Now, let's all go get in the truck, and we'll be on our way."

So off they went to the great Rocky Mountains of the West.

"Uncle Eric, why do they call these the Rocky Mountains? We were here earlier in the year to ski, and they didn't look so rocky to me," said Katie.

"When the pioneers first came to the West in the early discovery of this country, they came from the East, where the mountains were covered in trees. Don't you have lots of trees in your mountains of North Georgia?" said Eric.

"Yes," said Katie. "We have so many trees that you sometimes can't see the mountains for all the trees. And when we go all the way up Hickory Nut Mountain in Tallulah Falls, it looks like one big green carpet spread all over the hills. You can't see any ground because of all the trees."

"Well, when people came from those green mountains and got their first look at these mountains, they didn't just see trees; they saw big outcroppings of gigantic rock formations, so they named them the Rocky Mountains." said Uncle Eric. "And when you see where we are going, you will see what they call the tree line. That is the line above which no trees grow. It is so cold up that high, and the wind blows so hard, that trees just can't survive up there, so you can actually see a line along the side of the mountain where the trees stop growing."

The ride out of Denver to Vail Pass took about two hours. They went by small mountain towns where they could see gold mining taking place; they went into a big tunnel that went right through a mountain; they saw where giant rocks had fallen on the side of the road from far above them (and Katie hoped very much that no big rock would fall on them); they went by mountain lakes and rivers; and finally they climbed up a very steep road where she saw the sign that said, "Vail Pass, 10,567 feet." Here Uncle Eric took the exit off the highway, and they found themselves on a dirt road headed to Shrine Pass.

When they reached the very top of the road, Uncle Eric pulled into the parking lot and told everyone to get out and use the bathroom. It wasn't like any bathroom Katie had ever used. It was a small wooden room standing out all by itself, and instead of a flush toilet, it was just a seat that looked like a toilet, but with no running water. And when she looked into it, it was a long way to the bottom, and it was a smelly mess. She was very worried she might fall down into it and never get out, so she made her mom hold her hand the whole time. When she came out she told Uncle Eric he would have to do a lot better the next time if he wanted her to go to the bathroom, as she wasn't going to risk another one like that. They all just laughed at her, but she was serious, and she told Robert P. Rabbit so.

When everyone was ready, Katie thought they would just start their hike. But the trail that led up the mountain looked rather rough, and she was worried that her wheelchair would be hard to push on such uneven ground. But instead, Uncle Eric told everyone to get back into the car, and he took off down the dirt road for another half mile. When they stopped, there was a very small parking lot. But the trail

that led out of the parking lot had a sign with a picture of a wheelchair on it, and it was up this trail they all headed.

It is hard to describe the beauty of all Katie saw and experienced on this trail. There were fields of bright red wildflowers called Indian paintbrush and yellow asters blooming everywhere. There were purple flowers on tall thin stalks called lupine, and small blue and white ones called columbine. And after walking through the heavenly beauty of the wildflowers, they entered a forest of tall spruce and fir trees. The aroma was a lot like the pine forests at home, but the trees looked more like Christmas trees than tall Georgia pines.

After about a mile, they came to a large wooden deck that had been built right on the trail where they stopped to have their lunch. As they sat on the benches along the railing of the deck, Aunt Callie pointed out the mountain way in the distance that was called the Mount of the Holy Cross.

"They call it that because all year round the snow up on the side of the mountain never melts, and it lies in two gorges that intersect each other in the form of a cross." Katie looked up, and sure enough, there at the top of the mountain was a perfectly formed cross made of the gathered snow.

After they finished their lunch and were ready to go back, Katie looked around for Robert P. Rabbit, but he wasn't there. She called for him, but he didn't answer, nor did he appear.

"Oh, Uncle Eric," she cried. "We have to find him! He might get eaten by one of those coyotes or lions you told us about!"

"Don't worry, Katie," he said, "he couldn't have gone far. And this trail is so well traveled by people, I don't think the wild animals will come around it very much."

But Uncle Eric was more worried than he was letting on. Because some people leave food behind, the animals, even the mountain lions, will come around from time to time in hopes of finding some scraps. So he knew they needed to take some action right away. Along this trail there were signs that said that dogs must be kept on a leash, so Eric had Bridger on a leash to be sure he was obeying the rules. But drastic situations sometimes call for drastic measures, and this certainly was a drastic situation. Robert P. Rabbit might be safe in his home mountains of North Georgia, but he had never faced the dangers of the Rocky Mountains, so he had no idea what trouble he might be in right now.

"Callie," he said, "unleash Bridger and tell him to go look for Robert P. Rabbit." Bridger obeyed Callie better than anyone else, and if she spoke to him, he was more apt to mind than if Eric spoke to him.

"OK," said Callie, "but first let me have the blanket that is in your backpack, Katie, the one that Robert P. Rabbit was sleeping on."

So Katie gave the blanket to Aunt Callie, and she put the blanket in front of Bridger's nose and told him firmly, "Bridger, go find Robert P. Rabbit."

After getting a big whiff of the blanket, Bridger knew immediately what his mistress wanted. And since Robert P. Rabbit had become by far his most favorite friend in the animal world, he was off like a flash, hot on Robert P. Rabbit's trail.

In the meantime, while everyone ate their lunch on the deck, Robert P. Rabbit had decided to do a little exploring on his own. As they hiked up the trail earlier, he had noticed some wild strawberries growing close by, and he decided he would go back to find them for a little Rocky Mountain snack. It was a little further back than he had remembered, but he found them and was busily eating away, when suddenly he sensed danger near. He looked up, expecting to see a predator, a little angry with himself for not being more careful. He was prepared to take evasive action as his father had taught him, and as he had perfected many times in the North Georgia Mountains when confronted by a wild cat or a puma, but instead of what he expected, he saw something entirely different.

Surrounding him on all sides were four teenage boys with nothing but mischief on their faces.

"OK," the big one, who was obviously the leader, said. "We've got this rabbit surrounded, so I want each of us to start walking slowly toward him, and if he doesn't move, we will all jump on him at the same time. If he tries to run between any of us, use the club you are holding to hit him as hard as you can. It won't matter if you kill him, since we are going to cook him for dinner anyway."

Well, that didn't sound so good to Robert P. Rabbit, so he frantically tried to devise a plan of escape. He was having a very hard time doing so, since his situation seemed so hopeless. He thought there was a chance he could jump over the shortest one, but he needed a lot more room to get a running start for the jump. He also considered playing dead like he had seen his opossum friends do, and then as they let their guards down and reached down to pick him up, he would leap out of their reach. But that was an iffy proposition. He also thought about becoming inanimate to confuse them, but then he knew they would get hold of him, with very little chance of escape.

While all of this was running through his mind, an amazing thing happened. From out of nowhere came a tremendous growl so terrifying that it caused all four of the boys to scream at once and at the same time turn toward the sound to see what horrible creature was about to descend upon them.

Because their imagination was running wild, when they

saw a gigantic brown furry thing charging at them, all they could think of was "grizzly bear," and they threw down their clubs and ran for their lives.

Of course Robert P. Rabbit knew it was Bridger, and he was never so glad to see a dog in his entire life. Bridger skidded to a stop right over Robert P. Rabbit and stared menacingly after the boys just in case they got their courage back and decided to return. Of course, they were so frightened that they kept running as fast as they could down the trail, not daring to look back for fear that the grizzly was right behind them.

Bridger leaned down to lick Robert P. Rabbit, and then he let him hop up on his back and the two of them began to trot back to the others, who were coming down the path. When they came together, Robert P. Rabbit told Katie everything that had happened, and she related it to the others. Uncle Eric and Aunt Callie weren't sure that it really happened that way until they got back to the parking lot and heard the boys telling their parents all about the grizzly that had attacked them, and how they beat him off with clubs to save themselves.

Of course, Katie and Robert P. Rabbit knew they weren't telling the truth, so she made it a point to go over to where they were standing, leading Bridger, with Robert P. Rabbit on his back, right by them. They looked first at her, then at Bridger, and then at Robert P. Rabbit, and they knew that she knew they were telling a lie, but they could only stare as Katie and the others got into Uncle Eric's truck to leave.

On the way back, Katie slept the whole way, as the excitement of their first hike in the Rocky Mountains had certainly taken its toll. And Robert P. Rabbit insisted on curling up to sleep with Bridger to show his appreciation for his fast action in saving his life.

CHAPTER NINETEEN

THE PURLOINED PUMPKINS

It was the middle of October, and Katie and her mother were able to go back to Tallulah Falls since Katie had ended her treatment in Atlanta. Of course Katie couldn't go without Robert P. Rabbit, and since her mother had been told all about THE MARK and Robert P. Rabbit's amazing talents, and was now part of the privileged group of Robert P. Rabbit's friends, she had no objections to his coming along. In fact, she insisted on it.

As an added benefit, Katie was out of her wheelchair most of the time now, and the doctors said that they were now going to "watch and wait," which was music to Katie's ears. She was getting a little tired of hospitals and doctors. She appreciated everything they were doing to try to make her well, but she missed the North Georgia mountains and her little town of 160 people. It wasn't the Rockies where Aunt Callie, Uncle Eric, and Bridger were, but it was all she ever knew growing up, and she wanted to get back.

Besides, Katie, Will, and all of their friends were looking forward to Halloween. There was all the candy to think about, as well as deciding how they would dress up and where they would go trick or treating. But most of all, Katie was excited about carving a pumpkin into a scary face and helping her mom make her famous pumpkin pie.

As for Robert P. Rabbit, it was all a great mystery to him. He wondered what all the fuss was about. He had a million and one questions that Katie tried to answer as best she could.

"We go up to people's houses and ring the doorbell. When they answer, we yell out, 'TRICK OR TREAT.' If they give us a treat, then we won't play a trick on them. If they don't give us a treat, then we will trick them."

"That doesn't seem very nice. It sounds like bribery to me," said Robert P. Rabbit.

"Not really," said Katie. "It's all like playing a game, and everyone gets to join in. We really don't play any harmful tricks. We might ring their bell again and then run away, so that when they answer the door no one is there. Or maybe we might turn on their outside faucet where the hose is attached, and put the nozzle in the crook of a tree pointed at their window so that a steady stream of water hits their window, and they might think there is a big rain storm going on. We just do little tricks that might make them give some treats to the children who come by their house."

"Well, why does everyone dress up in funny costumes?" he asked.

"My dad said it started out that everyone dressed up so no one would recognize them if they played a trick. But now everyone dresses up just because it is a lot of fun and gives us something to look forward to on that wonderful night when we will get bags and bags of goodies," said Katie. "And just think, Robert P. Rabbit, you won't even have to put on a costume, 'cause you already are in a costume all the time," added Katie.

"Actually," he said, "I was thinking of dressing as a little human boy."

"Don't be so silly. Let's go out to the pumpkin patch and check on our special pumpkins," said Katie.

So off they went to the two-acre pumpkin patch that her father and mother, and many other parents in the community, work so hard on every summer. Each year a truck comes from Atlanta to buy all the pumpkins they can grow, which gives all the parents extra money to buy the children in Tallulah Falls new school clothes. The patch is close to the Tallulah River, in what they call Bottomland, so it grows really big pumpkins. And each year Katie and Will go to the patch and pick out their special pumpkins that they intend to use to carve into really funny, or scary, faces. Once they have picked out their pumpkins, they cut off all the other pumpkins growing near the special one, and that gives their pumpkins most of the nourishment coming along its vine from the ground.

This year Will and Katie both marked their special pumpkins by carving their initials near the stem on the pumpkins so there wouldn't be any mistake which ones were theirs.

As they arrived at the patch, Katie was in the lead and ran right to her pumpkin. At least she ran right to where her pumpkin should be, but it wasn't there.

"OH NO, Will!" she cried. "My pumpkin is gone. It's missing. It just isn't here at all!"

"Mine isn't here, either!" yelled Will.

"Maybe we're in the wrong place," said Robert P. Rabbit.

"No, we're not. This is exactly where our pumpkins should be. They were here a few days ago, 'cause I saw them when I came down with Mama," said Katie. "Someone has stolen our pumpkins."

"That will never do," said Robert P. Rabbit. "We will have to put our heads together and find out who has done this foul deed and report them to the police. So let's put our heads together and come up with a plan."

They began to work on their problem like all good de-tectives do. First they looked around for tracks. There hadn't been many people in the patch, as all the weeding and fer-tilizing had long since been completed. Besides, fall rains had washed away all but the most recent tracks. But lead-ing right up to their vine were the tracks of at least two peo-ple. One had farmer's boots on, with soles that had big cleats that made a definite impression in the moist dirt. The other looked much smaller and seemed to be the tracks of a tennis shoe, and they could see the word "Adidas," which was the same brand of tennis shoe that Katie's sister Arielle wore. But Katie was sure it was not Arielle's shoe, since she was still in Atlanta with Polly.

"Let's follow the tracks and see where they go," said Katie.

"It looks like they head toward the dirt road along the side of the patch," said Will.

So they followed the tracks to the dirt road that ran along the patch, and they could see that the tracks stopped.

"Wow, the tracks just stop right here," said Will.

"Yes, but look what else there is right where the tracks stop," said Robert P. Rabbit. "Aren't those tire marks?"

Sure enough, there in the road were the treads of a vehicle. It was obvious that at least two people, one a man and the other probably a boy or a woman, had driven to the patch in their truck, gotten out of the truck, come into the patch, and stolen their pumpkins. Then they had returned to the truck and driven away.

"Why would anyone steal someone else's pumpkins?" said Katie.

"That may be the clue to the whole mystery," said Robert P. Rabbit. "They either want the pumpkins for themselves, or they want them for another reason."

"I know," said Katie. "They want the pumpkins to sell so they will get money for them. This calls for special action. We need to go to Officer Goatcher."

Officer Goatcher is the Chief of Police in Tallulah Falls. It might be a small town, but it had to have a Chief of Police and one other police officer. Chief Goatcher was also the Chief of the Volunteer Fire Department for this part of North Georgia. He was a very busy man, so Katie wasn't sure he would be concerned about the theft of a couple pumpkins.

But they had to try, so off they went to City Hall, which consisted of a one-story building that housed the City Clerk, the Chief of Police, the hall where city meetings were held (and where Santa came for the Christmas party), and the Fire Department.

"Hi, Katie and Will," said Marcia, the City Clerk, when they walked in the door. "What can I do for you this fine day?"

"We need to report a crime," said Katie.

"Oh my goodness," said Marcia. "Has someone run a traffic light out on the highway?"

"No," said Katie. "There has been a theft, and we need Chief Goatcher to investigate."

At that moment, Chief Goatcher came out of his office and stood in the doorway. He was the biggest person that Katie knew, and just then he looked even bigger than she remembered. Some people in the town said he must have been an NFL linebacker, whatever that was, and Katie decided that if NFL linebackers were as big as Chief Goatcher, she didn't want to meet too many of them.

"Did I hear someone say that a crime has been committed?" said Chief Goatcher.

"Yes," said Will, who always liked talking to Chief Goatcher because some day he wanted to be on the Tallulah Falls police force, and talking to Chief Goatcher seemed like a good start toward that goal. "There has been a theft from our pumpkin patch. Someone has stolen our special pumpkins, and we think he should be arrested."

"How do you know it was a he?" asked the Chief.

"Because the tracks were too big for a woman, but there were some smaller ones that might be a woman. And they got away in a truck that left its tread tracks in the soft ground," said Will, almost out of breath.

"Well, you've been busy detectives," said the Chief. "It sounds like you are doing my job." Will looked proud. "This ought to make my job as a police officer a sure thing," Will thought.

"Come into my office and tell me everything else you know about this theft," said the Chief. So they went into Chief Goatcher's office and told him the story from beginning to end. The deputy wrote everything down as they talked.

"So you think you would know your two pumpkins if you saw them?" he asked.

"We sure would," said Katie. "The have our initials carved on them right where the stem comes into the pumpkin."

"OK," said the Chief. "You two go on home, and I'll be up later to talk to your parents."

"We're not in trouble, are we? " asked Katie.

"Certainly not," said the Chief. "But I want you to stay away from the pumpkin patch. Those people might come back, and I don't want you to be there if they do. That might be a dangerous crowd."

They left City Hall and walked the few blocks back home.

"I think Chief Goatcher knows more than he is letting on," said Robert P. Rabbit. "He wouldn't have brought in his deputy to write down what you were saying if he didn't think there was more to this story."

"What do you think it is?" asked Katie.

"I'm not sure, but whatever it is, I think he is going to need your help in catching these thieves," said Robert P. Rabbit.

After dinner, Katie's mom put her and Will to bed, but Robert P. Rabbit only pretended to be asleep at the foot of Katie's bed. He was pretty sure that when Chief Goatcher came, the conversation would be very interesting. Sure enough, a short time later there was a knock at the front door, and in walked Chief Goatcher.

"Good evening, Carl. Good evening, Wendy," he said. "Did your children tell you anything about our conversation this afternoon?"

"You mean that someone has taken their special pumpkins?"

"Yes," he said.

"They did tell us all about it. Do you think it is anything serious?" she asked.

"Yes, we do," he said. "In fact, your children aren't the only ones who have mentioned losing pumpkins. Several other farmers in the community have lost pumpkins from their fields. But we haven't had anything to go on until Katie told us about marking their pumpkins by carving their initials into the stems. This might give us the break we need to catch these people."

"What do you mean?" asked Carl.

"Well, if we can catch them with these particular pumpkins in their hands, we can arrest them. But Katie and Will would have to identify the pumpkins first," he said.

"How would they do that?" asked Wendy. "It seems a little dangerous."

"We've come up with a plan, but we need your permission first." He went on to explain his plan, and after much discussion, they agreed that if Katie and Will agreed, they would let the children help in catching the thieves.

Early in the morning, Robert P. Rabbit explained the entire plan to Katie and Will before they all went down to breakfast.

As they came running into the breakfast room, Will shouted, "Mom, Dad, me and Katie want to help the Chief catch the thieves. We think it is a good plan, and I know it will work, and we might even get a reward when they catch them!"

"How do you know what the plan is?" asked their mom.

"Because Robert P. Rabbit told us," said Will. This seemed to confuse Carl, but Wendy just looked at Robert P. Rabbit and let out a sigh.

"Well, OK, we will let you help the Chief, but we are going to go too. And Will, you don't do this for a reward, you do it because it is the right thing to do," she said.

The plan was pretty simple, but it did involve a little danger. Since it was Saturday, Chief Goatcher knew there was a farmer's market on the Rabun County Fairgrounds. Many of the local farmers brought their tomatoes, corn, beans, honey, watermelons, and especially pumpkins to be sold. Many people would be selling crafts, artwork, wood products, and everything you generally find at a fall fair.

Chief Goatcher intended to go by all of the stands selling pumpkins in hopes of finding Katie and Will's pumpkins. That would give him just enough evidence to arrest whoever was selling the pumpkins and enable him to gather further evidence.

When they got to the fair, they started making their rounds. Katie and Will were very excited. They were supposed to act like they were the Chief's children, and at many of the booths the Chief bought them candy apples, popcorn, cotton candy, and lots of other goodies. The Chief passed up all of the stands where he personally knew the farmers, as he knew they weren't the thieves. But there were at least three stands selling pumpkins where he didn't know the people.

At the first of these booths, he found out that the sellers were related to the wife of his deputy, so he passed them by. At the second stand, the woman behind the table said she was selling the pumpkins for the local hospital and that the pumpkins had been donated by a farmer whom the Chief knew personally, and so he passed that stand by.

But behind the third table were a man and a woman who the chief didn't know.

"Hi," he said. "Can my Katie and Will look at your pumpkins?"

Both of them looked very nervous, just like guilty people sometimes do when around an officer of the law.

"What for?" said the man.

"Why, to see if they want to buy one," said the Chief, no-ticing that the woman had a frown on her face. This cou-ple certainly wasn't acting anxious to sell pumpkins. They seemed quite unhappy that a policeman was standing on the other side of their table.

"Go ahead," said the man with a scowl on his face. "But they can't pick them up; they might drop them."

So Katie and Will began to walk around the pumpkins. Some were on the table, and some were on the ground. If they found either of the pumpkins, they were to tell the Chief that they wanted to buy them. The Chief would take over from there, and the children were to go back to where Wendy and Carl would be waiting.

As they walked around, Will was very nervous. Katie had to calm him down a couple times.

"Will, act natural," Katie said.

"I can't," said Will.

"Why not?" asked Katie.

"Because my pumpkin is over there, and I don't want one of these thieves to hit me over the head," he said.

"Will," Katie whispered, "show me where your pumpkin is."

So Will took Katie over to where the pumpkin was, and sure enough, Will's initials were right on that pumpkin, and Katie's was right next to Will's.

"Quick," said Katie, "we need to go tell the Chief."

With that, all kinds of confusion occurred. It all happened so fast that Katie felt someone was spinning her around. People were running every which way, and she didn't know where anyone was until she found herself being swept up into her mother's arms.

Later, Robert P. Rabbit told her what had happened.

Instead of quietly going back to tell the Chief that they had found their pumpkins, as soon as they saw Katie's pumpkin, Will started running toward the Chief, yelling at the top of his lungs, "We found the pumpkins! These are the thieves who stole our pumpkins. Arrest them! Arrest them! Put them in jail!"

The two thieves didn't wait to see what the Chief was going to do. They picked up some small pumpkins that were on their table and started throwing them at Chief Goatcher. Then they yelled to a third person who was sitting in a chair, "Get the truck! Get the truck! Hurry! Hurry!"

And then they took off running across the fairgrounds. The Chief blew his whistle, and from all sides of the fairgrounds policemen came running, police cars came closing in on the truck, sirens were going off, and people started running who knows where, and everything was a big mess for what seemed like thirty minutes, but was probably only five minutes.

After they cornered the truck, they arrested the three people, and when they searched the RV they were traveling in, they found many more pumpkins, some farm implements that had been stolen, and even some silver and jewelry that had been stolen from one farmer's house.

Later, at City Hall, Chief Goatcher, about seventy-five of the good people of Tallulah Falls, and some of the farmers who had had their produce stolen by these people gathered to have a celebration to honor Katie and Will. Of course Katie told them all that Robert P. Rabbit was a key part of their detective agency, and the crowd gave him a big round of applause while Katie held him in her arms.

As for Will, he didn't get a reward, but he got something better. Chief Goatcher gave Will a shiny badge to wear that said, "Town of Tallulah Falls Police" around the edge, and in the middle it said "Deputy." And ever since he got it, Will won't take it off. He even pins it on his pajamas when he goes to bed at night.

"Why don't you take it off at night?" his mama asked.

"Because you never know when Chief Goatcher might need me in the middle of the night, and I want to be sure I am ready with my badge on if that happens," he said.

And Robert P. Rabbit just winked at Wendy as she was turning out the light.

CHAPTER TWENTY

THE MYSTERY OF DIRT MAN, PART I

One of the best things about fall for our family has always been celebrating Thanksgiving. It is the time of year when we give thanks to God for all we have been given, and we come together as a family to decide who we will invite home to share the magnificent Thanksgiving dinner that Polly always prepares for us. Sometimes we invite widows from the church whose families are far away and who otherwise would be alone on Thanksgiving. Other times we invite a homeless family to come to our festive meal. Once we even invited the whole Chinese ping-pong (which they call table tennis) team that was playing an exhibition game at Taccoa Falls College near Tallulah Falls.

The funniest part of that day was when they found out we had a piano. It turned out that in addition to playing ping-pong, the group was also a choral group. We spent a good part of the afternoon learning Chinese songs. Our pronunciation was so bad that when we thought we were singing, "We love the early morning sun," what we were actually singing was, "Our frog is choking on the rice." Needless to say, the Chinese team enjoyed laughing at us.

Well, this year we all went up to Tallulah Falls for Thanksgiving. It was to be a year to top all years, as Katie, Will, and Parker were to meet someone who, up until then, they had only heard stories about, and quite frankly, were somewhat afraid of, although they weren't exactly sure why.

It all started a few days before Thanksgiving when Polly came in and announced, "There's going to be a meteor shower tonight."

"Oh, that's wonderful!" shouted Wendy. "We haven't had one of those in years."

"What's a meteor shower?" asked Katie.

"A meteor from outer space hits the upper atmosphere above the earth, and it catches on fire as it falls toward the ground. While it is falling, we can see it burning, and we call it a shooting star," said Wendy.

"Oh, I remember seeing shooting stars when we were out in Denver last summer," said Katie. "Will there be a lot of them tonight?"

"Well," said Polly, "tonight there will be hundreds of them hitting the atmosphere, but we won't be able to see most of them. They are too small, and they will be thousands of miles up in the sky. But we should see twenty or thirty of the larger ones, if we are lucky."

"What happens if they don't burn all the way up?" asked Will.

"Then they will hit the ground and end up in someone's field, or even on someone's house," said Wendy. "In fact, Mr. Lee found one in his garden a few years back."

"Was it still burning?" asked Will.

"No," said Wendy. "It had cooled off by the time he found it, so he could pick it up without any fear of getting burned. He could tell it was a meteor because it weighed ten times as much as a regular rock its same size. He gave it to the college, and they have it displayed in the lobby of their science building." She added, "But you don't need to worry. It is very rare for a meteor to make it all the way to the ground."

"Where will we go to see them?" asked Katie.

"The best place will be over in the middle of the pumpkin patch. There we will be away from the lights of the town and the road, and the trees won't interrupt our view of the whole sky. We'll take some blankets and pillows so we can lie on the ground and look up," said Wendy. "Besides," she added, "I need to take some eggs and jam to put into the bushel basket that hangs on the fence there, and to see if there are any flowers in it for me. I'm going to need some for our Thanksgiving table." The bushel basket was one of Wendy's private secrets the children were finally going to learn about before this holiday was over.

Anyway, Katie was excited about looking in the bushel

basket. It was fascinating to her that every time Mama took food and goodies to put into the bushel basket, the next day there were always flowers in it when they went back.

Later that morning, she was telling Robert P. Rabbit all about the meteor shower, and she happened to mention the bushel basket. Well, the meteor shower didn't excite Robert P. Rabbit at all. He told her that since he had lived out of doors all of his life, meteor showers were old hat to him. But the bushel basket was another thing altogether.

"Where is this mysterious bushel basket?" he asked.

"It is hanging on the fence post along the side of the pumpkin patch," she said. "When Mama puts homegrown food or eggs or fruits and vegetables in the basket, she swings it to the other side of the fence. Then whoever gets the food can see that there must be something it in for them, and they come and get it. Then, after they put something in the basket, they swing it to our side of the fence. Mama can see it from far away, and she knows it will have flowers or a carved piece of wood or some other handmade craft in it."

"Who is putting things in the basket?" he asked.

"Mama says it is Dirt Man, but I'm not too sure," she said. "We've always been afraid of Dirt Man. They say he captures little children and makes them cook his food and feed his animals, and do all kinds of other things for him before letting them leave and go home."

"Have you ever seen him?" asked Robert P. Rabbit.

"No," she said, "and I don't think I want to see him, either."

"That's silly," he said. "It's not fair to think all these bad things about him if you've never met him and have never given him a chance to tell you just who he really is. How did this all get started anyway?"

"I know," said Will, who had been listening to the whole conversation. "Mama was at the hardware store in town and she heard him tell Mr. Perkins that a fox had gotten all his chickens, and he didn't have any more eggs. So Mama told him she would be glad to give him some of our eggs. He said he would leave a bushel basket on the fence, and she could put the eggs in it. So she has been doing it for almost a year, and he keeps giving her things in return. Mama says he lives in the old army hut at the top of the field next to our pumpkin patch."

"Has she seen him again?" asked Robert P. Rabbit.

"I don't think so," said Katie. "But I think my daddy has. I saw him one day climbing over the fence with a rocking chair he had made for Dirt Man. He had to climb over the fence because Dirt Man never unlocks his gate for anyone. I think he is hiding something up there and doesn't want anyone to see it."

"Doesn't anyone live with him?" asked Robert P. Rabbit.

"Mama says he lives alone," said Katie, "and she says we are to leave him be. But he does have a strange donkey in his pasture. Whenever we go to the pumpkin patch to pick blueberries or the peaches and apples that grow around the sides of the patch, the donkey comes over to the fence and watches me. And when we are talking to each other, it surely looks like he is listening. I think he understands what we are saying. It's spooky."

"How would we get up to his hut?" asked Robert P. Rabbit.

"There is a road that goes along the fence that is the only way in or out," she said. "His pasture and the hut at the top are surrounded on three sides by the mountain that is owned by the government, and our land goes all the way across the bottom of his pasture. When he opens his gate to come out, he has to cross our pumpkin patch on the small dirt road we both use to get out to the main highway. Mama says the hut is what they call a Quonset Hut. It was used for officers to live in when soldiers were training on the mountain. Now it is Dirt Man's home."

"Why do they call him Dirt Man? Is that his real name?" asked Robert P. Rabbit.

"I don't know," said Katie. "Let's go ask Mama."

But just then Arielle came running into the room shouting, "Hurry! We need to get down to the bridge. A tractor-trailer truck has turned over and has spilled a load of watermelons all over the road. It's a real mess."

So off they all went as fast as they could. Arielle almost spilled Katie out of her wheelchair a couple times, and it was all Robert P. Rabbit could do to hold on for dear life.

Years ago, when a new road crew was building the highway across the bridge over the Tallulah River, they made a mistake. Just as the road leaves the bridge and starts up hill, it curves to the right, and right where it curves, they slanted the road down to the left, so that if a truck is going too fast, the weight in the top of the truck will lean way over to the left just as the truck is going to the right, and it simply turns over from the shift of weight. The wheels on the right side of the truck just come off the ground, and if the truck can't slow down quickly, over it goes.

Once a truck spilled a load of live chickens, and they ran every which way. Even today we see chickens in the bushes on the side of the road where they have been living in the

wild since they escaped the truck. And one truck was loaded with boxes of tennis balls that broke open, sending tennis balls up and down the highway. But worst was the day a
truck turned over carrying stacks of bee hives on its way to
the peach groves in South Georgia. No one except the bee
keeper could go near the truck for fear of being stung. It
was two days before the bees settled down and the tow truck
could haul the truck away.

When they got to the bridge, they saw watermelons everywhere. Some were rolling down the highway as people
tried to pick them up. But many of them had exploded, and
it was to these watermelons that Katie and her friends were
headed. Police Chief Goatcher was trying his best to keep
the kids away, but they all wanted to get their hands on as
much of the watermelon as they could. They were all eating watermelon and throwing pieces of watermelon at each
other, and some were even dropping big pieces of watermelon on the concrete just to see it break into pieces. By the
time Wendy arrived, Katie and Will had watermelon coming
down their chins, had watermelon all over their clothes, and
had watermelon all over Katie's wheelchair, and even all over
Robert P. Rabbit, who doesn't like watermelon much.

"Katie," said Wendy, "what in the world are you doing?
And Arielle, you should know better. Don't you know that
there could be germs on those watermelons? And you are in
the way. The tow truck is here, and they need to pick up this
turned over truck, and they certainly can't do that with you
all underfoot. Now let's get up on that bank and out of the
way. We can watch all the excitement from there. And put

down those dirty watermelons."

So for the rest of the afternoon they watched as the tow truck picked up the turned over truck and all the men from town helped put as many of the watermelons as they could back into the truck. As for Katie and Will, they had had all the watermelon they would want for an awfully long time. They couldn't even eat all their dinner, they were so full of watermelon. And right after dinner, they took a long nap until Wendy woke them up at about 10:00 p.m. This was later than Katie could ever remember being allowed to go outside, and she and Will were beside themselves with excitement.

It was not too far to the pumpkin patch. Arielle pushed Katie along the dirt road in what they called her travel chair. It was not at all as bulky as a big wheelchair and was much easier to handle on dirt roads. And some of the time, when Katie was feeling more balanced, she even walked along behind the travel chair pushing it herself.

About halfway down the winding driveway that runs from their house to the main road, they turned right onto what they call the farm road, and suddenly things looked much different. There was no moon that night, which Polly said would make it easier for them to see the shooting stars, and the trees began to take on the eerie shape of big, tall creatures. Katie was not sure about this meteor shower thing, and she got into her travel chair as quickly as she could, hugging Robert P. Rabbit tightly.

"Katie," said Robert P. Rabbit, "I think this is going to be a night to remember. And I don't mean the shooting stars."

"You're right," said Katie. "I feel that something important is going to happen."

And indeed it was.

CHAPTER TWENTY-ONE

THE MYSTERY OF DIRT MAN, PART II

Katie had not been down the farm road in so much dark-ness before. Usually when she went down the farm road at night, it was earlier in the evening, and every other time there had been a moon out to help light the way.

But this night there was no moon. There in the deep woods it was pitch black except for the flashlights Wendy had insisted they bring. The flashlights created giant shadows all around the big oak trees. A slight wind rustled the few leaves on the trees, which seemed to be swaying back and forth as they walked, giving the whole scene an eerie effect.

"I'm a little scared," whispered Katie to Robert P. Rabbit.

"Of what?" asked Robert P. Rabbit, although he was pretty certain he knew.

"It's the trees," said Katie. "They look so strange, like they are going to jump down on us."

"Katie," said Robert P. Rabbit. "Have you ever seen a tree move?"

"Well, no," said Katie.

"And you aren't ever going to, either. It doesn't matter if it is day or night; those trees are going to stay just where they are. They aren't going to jump or even crawl. If fact, they aren't going to move even one inch. They are stuck just where God let them grow. So you can stop worrying about the trees."

"OK," she said. "But I am still scared."

"What you are scared of, Katie? Are you scared because you don't know what is out there in the dark?"

"That's it, Robert P. Rabbit. You are really smart. I'm glad you're my friend, because not everyone would understand. What should I do?" she asked.

"Let's think about something else. You are thinking about things in your head that are not really there. If you think about a bear being out in the woods in the dark, then you are going to start worrying about the bear out in the woods in the dark. And since there isn't really a bear out in the woods in the dark, you will be worrying about a bear that never was there in the first place. So the best thing to do is just not think about the bear at all."

"Gee, Robert P. Rabbit, I wasn't thinking about a bear at all, but now that you have brought him up, I keep thinking about that bear, and now I'm worried that he is going to jump out and grab me. Do you think we should tell the others about the bear?"

"Oh Katie, I don't know what I'm going to do with you. We don't have to worry about that bear. Look, we just came out into the pumpkin patch, and the stars in the sky are beautifully bright. See, they light up the whole patch without even needing the moon to help," he said. "So let's just forget about the bear."

And sure enough, there they were, well out into the pumpkin patch. Wendy put down the blankets and pillows for them to lie on so they could look up at the meteor shower they all hoped would come.

"How long before we see the shooting stars, Mama?" asked Will.

"I don't know for sure, honey," she said, "but I think it won't be too long."

"OK," he said. "Katie, Robert P. Rabbit, and I are going to explore around the pumpkin patch and see what we can find."

"Don't go far, and stay inside the fence," she said.

"We will," said Katie, and off they ran to see what they had really wanted to see most this night, and that was Dirt Man's house.

"Let's get as close as we can," said Will. "If he is up there, I want to get a really good look at him. And we can stay behind the blueberry bushes. They will keep him from seeing us even when we get really close to his porch."

"I don't know, Will," said Katie. "I'm not sure I want to get too close. What if he gets angry at us for spying on him and comes after us with a pitchfork or something?"

"Don't worry, Katie," said Robert P. Rabbit. "I've got an idea. When we get close enough, I'll slip through the fence and hop up close to the porch to see if he is up there."

"You don't need to do that," said Will. "He's up there, all right."

"How do you know?" asked Katie.

"Don't you hear that noise?" he asked. "It's a squeaking noise, and its coming right from his porch."

"I hear it," said Robert P. Rabbit, "and I know what it is. Don't you remember telling us that your daddy made a rocking chair for Dirt Man? He is sitting in that rocking chair on his porch rocking back and forth, just as calm he pleases."

"Let's get a little closer and see if we can see him," said Will.

They crept as close as they could amongst the blueberry bushes until they were within a stone's throw of his porch.

"We need to just whisper from now on," said Katie, "or he might hear us."

"Listen," said Will. "He's talking to someone."

"How many are there?" said Dirt Man.

"There are eight of them," the other voice said.

"And what are they doing?" asked Dirt Man.

"I'm not sure, but they laid blankets down on the ground, and now they are lying on the blankets looking up into the sky," answered the voice.

"Well, why don't you just go on back along the fence and see what you can see, and then let me know what you think," said Dirt Man.

Katie, Will, and Robert P. Rabbit looked wide-eyed at one another. "We'd better go warn them," said Will. "We don't know who the other person is, or what he intends to do, and Mama and the others won't have any warning."

"Calm down," said Robert P. Rabbit. "Let's just go back and join the others. And don't say anything to anyone about what we have heard. Just leave it all to me. Do and say what I tell you to do and say."

So they hurried back to the others and took their places on the blankets, looking up as if nothing at all had happened out of the ordinary. A few minutes later, Arielle shouted,

"Look, the first shooting star!" After that there was a steady stream of shooting stars for the next forty-five minutes. They saw so many that they began to have a contest to see who could be the first to see the next one. Polly offered an ice cream cone the next day to whoever was first to see a shooting star the most times. Arielle saw the shooting stars first the most times, but she doesn't even eat that much ice cream. But no matter, it was an amazing night, with so many shooting stars that they lost count.

After a while it was time to go home, but they hadn't had a chance to tell anyone about seeing Dirt Man. Robert P. Rabbit said not to worry about it. He had snuck away from the blankets while they were all looking at the shooting stars and had gone to see just what was going on with Dirt Man, and he agreed that they should have a meeting the next day to discuss their next steps.

After breakfast the next day, Katie, Will, and Robert P. Rabbit went to their special fort to talk things over.

Running through the back of their yard in Tallulah Falls is a small creek, and beside the creek is a tall stand of bamboo. Their daddy cut a path into the bamboo and then cut out a square right in the middle of it where they can sit. The bamboo is so thick no one can see into it from the outside, so no one can bother them. This made a wonderful private place where they could meet and talk things over. They called it Fort Genius because they felt like real geniuses when they met there to make their plans about anything.

"OK," said Robert P. Rabbit. "Here's what happened the

other night. After we slipped out of the blueberry bushes and went back to our blankets, I hopped away to go over to the fence."

"I didn't see you do that," said Katie.

"That's because you were so intent on looking up into the sky," said Robert P. Rabbit. "When I got to the fence, I looked around to see who was talking to Dirt Man, the man he sent down to spy on us."

"Who was he?" asked Will.

"It wasn't a he; it was the donkey," said Robert P. Rabbit.

"The donkey?" said Katie in surprise. "What do you mean, the donkey?"

"I mean just what I said, the donkey," said Robert P. Rabbit. "I think the donkey is just like me, and that Dirt Man is just like you. They talk to each other. And Katie, when you felt like the donkey understood what you were saying when you all were in the pumpkin patch, you were right. He does understand you, and you can understand him. That's why you knew what he was saying when he talked to Dirt Man on the porch last night."

"What are we going to do about that?" asked Katie.

"Well," said Robert P. Rabbit, "I think we need to go back to Dirt Man's house to see if we can catch them taking again. But we need to do it when there is a full moon so we can see more, and we need to do it after dark so he will be less likely to see us."

So they spent the rest of the morning setting out their plan about how to catch Dirt Man talking to his donkey and what they would do when he realized they had caught him. But they had to wait a week until the next full moon to carry out their plan. It was awfully hard waiting—almost as hard as waiting for Christmas morning. But the night finally did come. It was the night before Thanksgiving.

"Mama," said Katie, "Will and I want to go to the pumpkin patch tonight to play. We'll go just as it gets dark, and we will be back in an hour."

"Katie, I can't let you two go out by yourselves in the dark. It's just not safe."

"But Mama," she said, "we'll have Robert P. Rabbit with us." Wendy just stared at Katie, not knowing what to say.

"I'll go with them," said Arielle.

"Well, OK, just so long as you are back one hour after sundown," said Wendy.

Katie and Will didn't really want Arielle to go with them, but they didn't have any other choice if they wanted to carry out their plan. So as they were on the way to the pumpkin patch, they explained to Arielle everything that had happened. Now Arielle doesn't have THE MARK below her right ear, so she has never heard Robert P. Rabbit speak. But

she has been around them so much now that she is a total be-
liever in the amazing Robert P. Rabbit. And besides, she had
always wanted to see Dirt Man, so she agreed to go along
with their plan.

"First we are going to find the donkey and Will is going
to feed him a big juicy apple. Then he will lead the donkey
to the porch where he will put down another apple for him,"
said Katie. "Then Robert P. Rabbit is going to hop up on
the porch and knock on the door. When he hears Dirt Man
coming to the door, he will hop away and rejoin us at the
fence. By then the donkey should be eating the apple we will
leave on the porch, so he should be there when Dirt Man
comes to the door. Then they will start talking, and we can
all shout out that we hear them and know what they are saying," she added.

"What happens then?" asked Arielle.

"We don't know," said Robert P. Rabbit. "We will cross
that bridge when we come to it."

By then they had reached the fence. But before Will could
go through the fence with the apple, they noticed that the
donkey was already standing at the porch. He had a saddle
on his back, and across the saddle horn was a brightly lit lantern. They all crept carefully along the fence until they were
as close to the porch as they could get. When they were nearly close enough to throw a pebble at the donkey and hit him,
they heard the donkey speak in a low, eerie voice.

"Dirt Man. Dirt Man. 'Stime to go." And then again,
"Dirt Man. Dirt Man. 'Stime to go."

They were terrified. The donkey sounded so ominous that they just froze. Robert P. Rabbit didn't try to hop up to knock on the door, and Will certainly didn't try to give the donkey an apple.

A third time the donkey said, "Dirt Man. Dirt Man. 'Stime to go."

The door suddenly opened. Dirt Man came out onto the porch and stepped into the saddle on the back of the donkey. The donkey slowly turned, hesitating as he faced them, and for an instant they were sure he saw them. But then he kept on turning, and off down the dirt road he went with Dirt Man on his back and the lantern swinging from the saddle horn.

"What shall we do?" asked Katie.

"Let's follow them," said Robert P. Rabbit.

"I'm for that," said Will.

And before Arielle could say a thing, off down the fence line went Robert P. Rabbit, with Will pushing Katie in her travel chair close behind. Arielle didn't have any choice but to follow. When they got to the end of the fence line, Dirt Man opened the gate and went through.

"Where do you think they are going?" asked Katie.

"It looks like they are headed to the church to me," said Will.

And sure enough, as soon as the donkey got to the church, he turned up into the dirt driveway and walked around behind the church.

"I don't think I want to follow him anymore," said Katie. "It's scary back there. That's where the graveyard is. We won't go farther than the side of the church. We can see everything we want to see from there."

So they turned up the driveway and slowly worked their way along the Church to the back corner of the building where they stopped.

"I don't see the lantern anymore," said Katie. "Let's go back home. I don't like this."

"Wait a minute," said Will. "I see the light. It's right over there in the garden, next to those vines."

"You're right, Will. There's the donkey, but Dirt Man is no longer in the saddle. I wonder where he's gone?" said Katie.

"Why don't you turn around and see for yourself?" a voice suddenly said from behind them.

"It's him! It's him! Run! Run!" shouted Will, running toward the back of the church.

"Stop!" cried Katie. "I don't think we are in danger. I think he wants to talk to us."

As Will came back to hide behind Katie, they looked carefully at the person in front of them. What they saw was a man with a gentle face and a smile that put them at ease. He wasn't much taller than Katie, but he had large hands—hands of a person who had done a lot of hard work. He held a garden spade in his right hand and a small flowering plant in his left. His shirt and pants were covered with dirt as if he had been on his knees working in the ground, and he was wearing work boots like the kind their father wore when he is weeding their garden or cutting trees around their house. His skin was dark, and not just because he had been in the sun a lot, but because he was made that way.

"Isn't that so, Dirt Man? Am I right?" she asked.

"Yes, Katie, you are correct," he said. "I have been wondering why you have been spying on me, and I am especially curious about the fact that Jeremiah says you can understand him and even talk to him if you wanted to."

"Who is Jeremiah?" asked Katie.

"That is my donkey," he said. "I don't know why I have been able to talk to him, and why he can talk to me, except that I found one place in the Bible where a donkey talked to Jeremiah, so I named him Jeremiah."

By then Will had settled down, and Arielle was taking it all in as if she were a reporter who was going to write a story for the paper.

"He can talk to you, and you to him, because you have

THE MARK," said Robert P. Rabbit, who went on to explain about why Katie and Will could do the same thing and why he, Dirt Man, could communicate with Jeremiah.

Dirt Man seemed surprised that a rabbit was talking to him and seemed to understand what he was saying. "Oh, now we have a talking rabbit, do we?" he said. "What will it be next, talking pigs?"

"No," said Robert P. Rabbit. "Pigs will never talk. They are too busy eating and making pigs of themselves to bother talking."

They spent the next hour talking and talking about everything that had happened to them since they met Robert P. Rabbit. They even had a chance to talk to Jeremiah and listen to his story, which is a story for another time.

Dirt Man listened very politely until finally Will asked, "Why did you come to the graveyard at the church?"

"Oh, I am in charge of planting the flowers around the graveyard and around all of the church, and this year I planted a moonflower vine. It only blooms at night, and it blooms especially well at the time of the full moon. Tonight is the full moon, so Jeremiah reminded me that it was time to see the blooms. So here I am, and here you are too. Would you like to see them?"

"Oh yes," said Katie. "And we'd like to see all your other flowers too, if you'll let us."

"Certainly I will. You can come over anytime and I'll show you all my garden. It is behind my hut, so no one can really see it unless I bring them back. I would love to take you back there. I've invited your mother, and she says she will come one day when she isn't so busy."

"That reminds me," said Katie, "why do you and Mama put the things in the bushel basket? Why doesn't she bring the fruits and vegetables and eggs right up to your house?"

"Well, it's quite simple. You see, if she came all the way up to the house, she would first have to go all the way down to the gate, open it up, walk all the way up to the hut, then walk all the way down to the gate again and back up to the farm road. It's just a lot easier to use the bushel basket," he said.

That made a lot of sense to Katie, but she was a little disappointed that it wasn't something a little more mysterious.

Finally, Will asked him the question they were all wondering, but had been afraid to ask. "Is Dirt Man your real name?"

"No," he said. "When I first came to the mountains of Tallulah Falls, I was running away from some sadness. I'll tell you all about it sometime. I wanted to be alone, so I just didn't talk to anyone. I found the hut through some friends of mine in the government, and it suited my wishes for privacy perfectly. So when I went to town, I didn't speak any more than I had to—just did my business and came back home. I didn't tell anyone my real name, as they probably wouldn't be able to pronounce it, and, since I am always working in my garden and generally am covered with soil when I go to town, they started calling me Dirt Man, and I let them do so."

"But I'll tell you my real name," he went on, "since we are going to be friends, and since you understand that I'm not crazy talking to Jeremiah. My name is Haprid Sanjeeve, and you can call me Hap."

"Hap," said Katie thoughtfully. "I like that name!"

"Isn't your mother going to worry about you all being out this late at night?" he asked.

"Oh dear," said Arielle, "I promised to have you back in an hour, and it's been over two hours. I think I'm in real trouble."

"Here," said Dirt Man. "I'll push Katie and carry Will on Jeremiah so you can make better time getting home. Let's go!"

They went off as quickly as they could, and soon they were coming into their driveway when they saw Chief Goatcher's police car up at the house with the blue light going round and round frantically, like it did when he stopped speeders on the highway. Somehow they all knew that he was there because of them not coming home when they said they would, so they came up the driveway with a certain amount of fear and trembling, sure Mama would be very angry at them.

But instead of being angry, Wendy just ran down the driveway with her arms open, crying tears of joy. She gave them all hugs and kisses and thanked Chief Goatcher for coming to help. After she heard the whole story, she thanked Dirt Man profusely and insisted that he come to Thanksgiving dinner the next day, which he did.

So from then on Katie, Will, Robert P. Rabbit, and Hap became the best of friends, and Hap became a very important part of the Global Detective Agency. As for Jeremiah, while he could talk to them, and they to him, he was not the brightest light bulb in the lamp, so he was not taken into the inner circle of their friendship, but was allowed to tag along from time to time.

CHAPTER TWENTY-TWO

A CHRISTMAS LESSON

Thanksgiving dinner was a wonderful affair, with Hap telling us his whole story about coming from India as a young man to attend school at Georgia Institute of Technology. He met his wife there, and they both went to work for a computer company in Atlanta where they spent many hours writing software for other companies. They couldn't have children, so they volunteered at the Boys and Girls Clubs of Atlanta, and they were able to watch many children grow up in the clubs and then go off to college or trade school to become good citizens and parents.

But a few years ago he lost his wife in a terrible auto accident, and he began to lose interest in his job because he and his wife always did the work together. Without her, the work wasn't as much fun. His boss was very understanding and knew some people in the military who made the hut in Tallulah Falls available to him, so he came up here to be alone. He still works for the company, though, and little by little they have been sending work to him that he can do on his computer at home.

In fact, he had so much fun with our family, both at Thanksgiving and later during a fun afternoon sledding together, that he invited us all to his hut for some hot chocolate. While we were there, he took us into what he calls his Command Center. It is a climate-controlled room in the back of the hut that is filled with computers, monitors, keyboards, and electronic equipment that you only see in movies, or that you might see in the control tower of a busy airport. Katie and Will later said they think he really works as a spy for the CIA.

While they were in the hut with Hap, Katie, Will, and Robert P. Rabbit asked him if he would agree to be a part of their Global Detective Agency, and he said the next time they had a case to solve, they should come to him for help. Then, if he felt that they were sincere, honest, and efficient in their handling of the case, he would officially join them. They were so excited that Will said they should put out a flier in the neighborhood advertising that they could solve cases and asking people to bring their unsolved mysteries to them. But Katie said that wouldn't be dignified and that they should just wait until the right case came along.

A week or so later, a case did, in fact, come along.

Every year, a month or so before Christmas, Wendy goes to the public room at City Hall to teach sewing. In the mountains, the people who live there year-round don't always have a lot of money to spend. In fact, this year there was what the grown-ups called a Depression, and many of the men in the area had lost their jobs. So the ladies came to the class to sew some presents for their families. In years past they have made shirts, trousers, coats, and even blankets that they made from big pieces of fabric that Carl found at a flea market. Wendy showed the ladies how to sew trim all around the edges so they were just as good as you can get at a store.

Well, this year, Carl was able to find a giant box of skeins of yarn. Wendy explained that a skein is a big bundle of yarn not yet rolled into a ball. So she went to the store and bought lots and lots of knitting needles, and she told the ladies that instead of sewing things, this year they were going to knit hats, scarves, and gloves. She thought about knitting sweaters, but she decided that the ladies weren't ready for something that complicated, and besides, there just wasn't enough time to do that.

City Hall is right next to the big yard where there are bluegrass concerts for the community from spring to fall. After Thanksgiving, the bluegrass ends and the kids in town take over the entire area for their own private play yard. On this pleasant afternoon Will, Katie, and Robert P. Rabbit were building a fort using the cardboard box that the skeins had come in, plus some other cardboard boxes they found at the back of City Hall.

"Wow," said Will. "We have the only three-room fort ever to be built in the history of Tallulah Falls. I'm going to use my pocket knife to cut some windows in the sides of the fort so we can see any enemies that might come to attack."

"Will, we don't have any enemies," said Katie. "We only have friends."

"You never know when some of your friends might become enemies," said Will.

"I certainly hope not," said Katie. "But I like the idea of windows anyway, so we can see when our friends are coming to visit us."

The windows were cut in the sides of the cardboard, and sure enough they saw some people as they looked through the window that gave them a view of City Hall.

"Look over there at the back of City Hall," said Katie. "Aren't those the Hatcher twins?"

The twins were the children of widow Hatcher, who lived up on the mountain in a place overlooking the Tallulah Gorge that had been there for many years. In fact, it had been there unoccupied for so long that everyone forgot who it belonged to. When Mrs. Hatcher came to town looking for a place to stay with her two twelve-year-old girls, the men in the town fixed up the basement of the old house, and she moved right in. People hadn't gotten to know them very well yet, as they had been in Tallulah Falls for not even a whole year.

"Yeah," said Will, "and they are looking mighty suspicious. I think they are spying on someone as they are looking through the back window. It looks like they don't want to be seen from the inside. See? Their heads are barely above the windowsill."

"Do you think we should tell someone?" asked Katie.

"No," said Will. "Let's watch a little longer and see what they are going to do. And Robert P. Rabbit, we need you to hop over there to get a closer look. It's hard to see from here, and you might be able to tell what's going on."

So over he hopped, trying to stay as inconspicuous as possible. He stayed under the small bushes along the back of the property. When he reached the twins, he darted across the open ground and under the very bush beside which they were standing. A few minutes later he came hopping back to the fort. They huddled in the corner of the fort and discussed all he had seen. They decided to look out the window again, but when they did, the girls were gone.

"If there is something illegal going on, my guess is that they will be back again tomorrow, so let's be sure we are here. In the meantime, Katie, find out everything you can about the twins. When we get all our facts together, we'll go see Hap and see if he can help us solve this mystery," said Robert P. Rabbit.

That night at dinner, Katie said, "Mama, what do you know about the Hatcher sisters?"

"I know that they are twins, and they are about twelve or thirteen years old," said Wendy.

"Is that all you know?" asked Will.

"Well, I know that they live with their mother in the basement of the Overlook Building and that they don't have a father living with them," she said.

"Why would anyone want to live in the basement of the Overlook Building?" asked Will. "It can't be very big, and the building is kind of old, isn't it?"

"Will, some people don't have as much money as we do, so they can't live in a house like we can. They just have to do the best they can with what they have, and I suppose the basement of the Overlook Building is all they can afford right now," she said.

"Doesn't their mother have a job?" asked Katie.

"Yes, she cleans City Hall every day. And she does a wonderful job of it, I might say. Better than anyone we have ever had since your father became mayor. She doesn't make a lot of money, but she is able to put her girls on the school bus in the morning here in town and be here when they get home," she added.

The next day, the three of them were back in their fort in the afternoon after school, and sure enough, there were the twins hiding under the bushes and looking into the window just like the day before. Only this time they were ducking down from time to time whispering to each other and working on something, and then standing up again to look into the window.

Robert P. Rabbit went back over to the bush where he could see more of what was going on, and he came back with new information. "I think we have enough information to go to Hap to see what he can help us with. This mystery may not be that hard to solve from what we know now, but there is something about it all that bothers me, and I'm just not sure what it is," he added.

So they hurried to the pumpkin patch and through the hole they had cut in the fence to see Hap at his hut.

After they knocked on the door, they heard his voice from the back room. "Come in, Katie, Will, and my good friend Robert P. Rabbit."

"How did you know it was us?" asked Will as they went into the hut.

"It's my business to know what other people don't know," said Hap. "Besides, I saw you on this monitor from the minute you passed under my fence," he said, pointing to one of the big screens on the wall. "Now, tell me what has brought you my way this fine day."

"We have a mystery we need your help with," said Katie.

"OK," said Hap. "First I want you to tell me all the facts that you know so far. Then, from the facts, we'll see if we can tell what the real problem is."

"OK, here is what we know so far," said Katie, looking down at the notebook where she had taken careful notes.

"Mrs. Hatcher is poor. She lives in the basement of the Overlook Building. She has twin girls twelve or thirteen years old. She is a good cleaning woman, cleaning City Hall every day. And every day the twin girls come to the back of City Hall and look through the window into the building, and then duck behind the bush to do something, and then look through the building again.

"When Robert P. Rabbit hopped over to see what they were doing, he saw that they were knitting something. But they were using multi-colored yarn that they had tied together, so they weren't doing a very good job of it. And, oh yes, Mama holds a knitting class everyday for the women who want to come and knit things for Christmas for their families, like gloves and scarves," added Katie.

"The knitting classes are free," said Will. "So we don't understand why they don't just go in with the other women and knit like everyone else. We think maybe they are up to something bad, but we just can't figure out what it is."

"Is that all?" asked Hap.

"I think so," said Katie sheepishly, pretty sure there must be something else they should know, but not certain what that might be.

"OK, here is what I think the facts show. First, the girls are too poor to buy their mother presents for Christmas at the store, or they have just decided that they want to make their mother Christmas presents rather than buy them. Next, they don't know how to knit, so they are taking the knitting lessons through the window, rather than going inside," he said.

"Why wouldn't they just go inside?" asked Will.

"I know," said Robert P. Rabbit. "Their mother works there, and they don't want her to know what they are making her for Christmas. That was what was bothering me, and now I know what it was."

"Bingo!" said Hap. "You hit the nail on the head. And they are probably using multi-colored yarn tied together because they have had to use the pieces of yarn that the other women cut off, and which are thrown away each night. They must be getting the yarn pieces from the trash and tying them together to do their knitting. Will, they aren't doing anything wrong, but they certainly are going to find it very hard to complete anything for their mother that way," said Hap. "So, my little detectives, what are you going to do about this mystery?"

"I want to help them," said Katie.

"And how do you propose to do that?" asked Hap.

"First, we need to get them a whole skein of yarn in each color they want. Then we need to find a place where they can knit that isn't outside under that window. Why, if it rains, they can't knit at all," said Katie.

"And then we need to help them find pretty boxes, and ribbon and wrapping for the presents," added Will.

"And I think you are going to have to join them in this little project, which means that if you aren't knitting now, you need to start," said Hap.

"You mean we need to knit something for their mom?" asked Will.

"No," said Hap. "I mean that you need to knit something for your mother, and you need to do it with them."

"But we don't know how to knit," said Will.

"Then here's where you have to use a little friendly deception. First you go to your mom and tell her that you want to knit something for Parker and Arielle, and that you want to come to the knitting class to learn how to do it. Then, each day you get a lesson, and when it is finished you go somewhere to meet the twins and show them what you learned that day. And you can bring them as much yarn as they need to do their knitting. How does that sound?" asked Hap.

"That sounds like a plan," said Robert P. Rabbit.

So that night they told Wendy that they wanted to come to the knitting class to learn to knit. Unknown to them, Hap had called Wendy and told her all about what was happening, so she was able to add a few things that would make the project very special.

"Katie," she said, "why don't you use Polly and Grand-Dad's cottage to do your knitting in the afternoon? You are a little bit behind the others in the class, so you can do your catching up in the cottage. And I will give you lots of extra yarn so you can make more than one thing if you want."

What a grand idea that was. GrandDad and Polly's cottage was right next door, but it had a side entrance where the twins could come in without being seen.

The next day, as soon as the twins got off the bus, Katie and Will went over to them to talk. When they told the twins that they had seen them at the window each day, the twins were at first really worried. But Katie told them that they wanted to knit things for their family and that they had a plan that would help them all. When she told them her plan, they were very excited and agreed that it was the best plan ever.

After that class, and after every class for the next several weeks, they spent hours and hours together in Grand-Dad and Polly's cottage just knitting their hearts away. And when they had to tell Polly what they were doing, because she and GrandDad had come up to get ready for Christmas in Tallulah Falls, Polly was a big help. She had been knitting for years, and she was able to get them over some of the more difficult parts on knitting things, especially the fingers of a glove.

A few days before Christmas, Katie came to Wendy and said, "Mama, the twins tell us that they won't have a Christmas tree this year. And they said that they only give each other one present Christmas morning. That seems so sad. Can't we buy them some more presents?"

"Katie, that is a wonderful thought on your part, but we shouldn't do that. It would make their mother feel very bad that she couldn't do more for her girls, while someone else could. I have another idea. Why don't we invite them to our house Christmas morning for all of us to open our presents together? Then they can have Christmas dinner with us and can go with us when we take the town presents to the shut-ins and widows. I'll talk to their mother tomorrow at City Hall. I'm sure she would be glad to help."

"But Mama," said Katie, "we always have so many presents for each other that they might feel bad only having one thing."

"Katie," she said, "your father and I have talked about it, and this year we want to draw names, and each of us will only give a present to one other person in the family. That way we will each have one present to open."

Well, that worked out very well for Katie, because as hard as she tried, she had only been able to knit one scarf. So she had her one present to give. And she was sure that Will was only able to knit one wool hat.

The next day, Katie saw Wendy deep in conversation with Mrs. Hatcher, and when they were finished talking, Mrs. Hatcher gave Wendy a long hug.

It was the best Christmas ever. The twins and their mother came early, and everyone was very anxious to open their present. GrandDad read the Christmas story from the book of Luke and explained to everyone that just as God gave us the one gift of Jesus, we each were going to receive one gift for Christmas. Wendy loved the scarf Katie knitted for her; Parker liked the hat Will made for him so much that he wore it around all day, even in the house; and Carl said the gloves Wendy knitted for him were the best ever.

But two people broke the rule. Both twins gave their mom something they had knitted. She got a pair of gloves and a scarf. But nobody minded, and we all joined in singing Christmas carols while Wendy played the piano.

Then we all went down to City Hall and got the presents that the City Council had purchased for the deserving people in the community. The twins, their mom, Will, and Katie served as the main delivery people for the gifts. We sang Christmas carols at each house and got lots of hugs. What a wonderful time it was. With all the action, Christmas dinner didn't take place until that evening, but that was OK, because everyone was so hungry there wasn't anything leftover, so we didn't have much to clean up afterwards.

That night as Katie and Robert P. Rabbit were snuggled up ready to go to sleep, Katie asked, "Robert P. Rabbit, wasn't that the best Christmas ever?"

"It certainly was," he said. "Since it was my first Christmas ever, I guess it was the best. But then again, since it was my only Christmas ever, I guess it was my worst too."

"Oh, you're silly," said Katie, and she closed her eyes and fell asleep in two minutes.

AUTHOR'S NOTE

Since my granddaughter, Katie, lives in Tallulah Falls, Georgia, where the nearest hospital is over forty-five minutes away, she came to live with us during her treatments; we live only five minutes from Children's Healthcare of Atlanta. As she was going through her procedures, I read to her for many hours each day. However, since I was not able to find books where the hero or heroine of the story is a child who is sick or in a wheelchair, I ended up telling her story after story where she and her brother Will were the heroes. They were always accompanied by Robert P. Rabbit. It wasn't long before she wanted a new Robert P. Rabbit story every day, and I always accommodated her.

I hope that these stories will help the sick children you know, and those who are in a wheelchair or are in bed, realize that even with a disability, they can enjoy the life they have been given.

For more information about the Robert P. Rabbit series of books, or to find order information for the books, go to our web site—*www.robertprabbit.com*—or to one of our Facebook pages—*Robert P. Rabbit* or *The Larry Burkett Foundation*.